"He's *mine*, isn't he?" Rohan ground out. His tone was implacable.

Charlotte wasn't up to this. She was a lost soul. She was acutely aware of the pronounced pallor beneath Rohan's golden-olive skin. He was in shock too. She wanted to touch his face. Didn't dare. She felt sorrow. Guilt. Pity. Remorse. Her heart was fluttering like a frantic bird in her breast. She had to work out how to deal with the whole momentous issue. She needed time to *think*. She allowed a fallen lock of hair to half shield her face.

"Isn't that why you're trembling from head to foot?" he asked curtly. "Christopher is *mine*. My child."

WEALTHY AUSTRALIAN, SECRET SON

BY
MARGARET WAY

First published in Great Britain 2011
Harlequin Mills & Boon Limited,
Eton House, 18-24 Paradise Road, Richmond, Surrey TW9 1SR

© Margaret Way, Pty., Ltd 2011

ISBN: 978 0 263 21939 5

Harlequin Mills & Boon policy is to use papers that are natural, renewable and recyclable products and made from wood grown in sustainable forests. The logging and manufacturing process conform to the legal environmental regulations of the country of origin.

Printed and bound in Great Britain
by CPI Antony Rowe, Chippenham, Wiltshire

Margaret Way, a definite Leo, was born and raised in the subtropical River City of Brisbane, capital of the Sunshine State of Queensland. A Conservatorium-trained pianist, teacher, accompanist and vocal coach, she found her musical career came to an unexpected end when she took up writing—initially as a fun thing to do. She currently lives in a harbourside apartment at beautiful Raby Bay, a thirty-minute drive from the state capital, where she loves dining *al fresco* on her plant-filled balcony, overlooking a translucent green marina filled with all manner of pleasure craft: from motor cruisers costing millions of dollars, and big, graceful yachts with carved masts standing tall against the cloudless blue sky, to little bay runabouts. No one and nothing is in a mad rush, and she finds the laid-back village atmosphere very conducive to her writing. With well over one hundred books to her credit, she still believes her best is yet to come.

CHAPTER ONE

The present

IT WAS an idyllic day for a garden party. The sky was a deep blue; sparkling sunshine flooded the Valley; a cooling breeze lowered the spring into summer heat. A veritable explosion of flowering trees and foaming blossom had turned the rich rural area into one breathtakingly beautiful garden that leapt at the eye and caught at the throat. It was so perfect a world the inhabitants of Silver Valley felt privileged to live in it.

Only Charlotte Prescott, a widow at twenty-six, with a seven-year-old child, stood in front of the bank of mirrors in her dressing room, staring blindly at her own reflection. The end of an era had finally arrived, but there was no joy in it for her, for her father, or for Christopher, her clever, thoughtful child. They were the dispossessed, and nothing in the world could soothe the pain of loss.

For the past month, since the invitations had begun to arrive, Silver Valley had been eagerly anticipating the Open Day: a get-to-know-you garden party to be held in the grounds of the grandest colonial mansion in the valley, Riverbend. Such a lovely name, Riverbend! A private house, its grandeur reflected the wealth and community standing of the man who had built it in the 1880s, Charles

Randall Marsdon, a young man of means who had migrated from England to a country that didn't have a splendid *past*, like his homeland, but in his opinion had a glowing *future*. He'd meant to be part of that future. He'd meant to get to the top!

There might have been a certain amount of bravado in that young man's goal, but Charles Marsdon had turned out not only to be a visionary, but a hard-headed businessman who had moved to the highest echelons of colonial life with enviable speed.

Riverbend was a wonderfully romantic two-storey mansion, with a fine Georgian façade and soaring white columns, its classic architecture adapted to climatic needs with large-scale open-arched verandahs providing deep shading for the house. It had been in the Marsdon family—*her* family—for six generations, but sadly it would never pass to her adored son. For the simple reason that Riverbend was no longer theirs. The mansion, its surrounding vineyards and olive groves, badly neglected since the Tragedy, had been sold to a company called Vortex. Little was known about Vortex, except that it had met the stiff price her father had put on the estate. Not that he could have afforded to take a lofty attitude. Marsdon money had all but run out. But Vivian Marsdon was an immensely proud man who never for a moment underestimated his important position in the Valley. It was *everything* to him to keep face. In any event, the asking price, exorbitantly high, had been paid swiftly—and oddly enough without a single quibble.

Now, months later, the CEO of the company was finally coming to town. Naturally she and her father had been invited, although neither of them had met any Vortex representative. The sale had been handled to her father's satisfaction by their family solicitors, Dunnett & Banfield. Part of the deal was that her father was to have tenure of the Lodge—originally an old coach house—during his lifetime, after which it would be returned to the estate. The coach house had been converted and greatly enlarged by her grandfather into a beautiful and comfortable guest house that had enjoyed a good deal of use in the old days, when her grandparents had entertained on a grand scale, and it was at the Lodge they were living now. Just the three of them: father, daughter, grandson.

Her former in-laws—Martyn's parents and his sister Nicole—barely acknowledged them these days. The estrangement had become entrenched in the eighteen months since Martyn's death. Her husband, three years older than she, had been killed when he'd lost control of his high-powered sports car on a notorious black spot in the Valley and smashed into a tree. A young woman had been with him. Mercifully she'd been thrown clear of the car, suffering only minor injuries. It had later transpired she had been Martyn's mistress for close on six months. Of course Martyn hadn't been getting what he'd needed at home. If Charlotte had been a loving wife the tragedy would never have happened. The *second* major tragedy in her lifetime. It seemed very much as if Charlotte Prescott was a jinx.

Poor old you! Charlotte spoke silently to her image. *What a mess you've made of your life!*

She really didn't need anyone to tell her that. The irony was that her father had made just as much a mess of his own life—even before the Tragedy. The *first* tragedy. The only one that mattered to her parents. Her father had had little time for Martyn, yet he himself was a man without insight into his own limitations. Perhaps the defining one was unloading responsibility. Vivian Marsdon was constitutionally incapable of accepting the blame for anything. Anything that went wrong was always someone else's fault, or due to some circumstance beyond his control. The start of the Marsdon freefall from grace had begun when her highly respected grandfather, Sir Richard Marsdon, had died. His only son and heir had not been able to pick up the reins. It was as simple as that. The theory of three. One man made the money, the next enlarged on it, the third lost it. No better cushion than piles of money. Not every generation produced an heir with the Midas touch, let alone the necessary drive to manage and significantly enlarge the family fortune.

Her father, born to wealth and prestige, lacked Sir Richard's strong character as well as his formidable business brain. Marsdon money had begun to disappear early, like water down a drain. Failed pie-in-the-sky schemes had been approached with enthusiasm. Her father had turned a deaf ear to cautioning counsel from accountants and solicitors alike. He knew best. Sadly, his lack of judgement had put a discernible dent in the family fortunes. And that was even before the Tragedy that had blighted their family life.

With a sigh of regret, Charlotte picked up her lovely hat with its wide floppy brim, settling it on her head. She rarely wore her long hair loose these days, preferring to pull it back from her face and arrange it in various knots. In any case, the straw picture hat demanded she pull her hair back off her face. Her dress was Hermes silk, in chartreuse, strapless except for a wide silk band over one shoulder that flowed down the bodice and short skirt. The hat was a perfect colour match, adorned with organdie peonies in masterly deep pinks that complemented the unique shade of golden lime-green.

The outfit wasn't new, but she had only worn it once, at Melbourne Cup day when Martyn was alive. Martyn had taken great pride in how she looked. She'd always had to look her best. In those days she had been every inch a *fashionista*, such had been their extravagant and, it had to be said, *empty* lifestyle. Martyn had been a man much like her father—an inheritor of wealth who could do what he liked, when he liked, if he so chose. Martyn had made his choice. He had always expected to marry her, right from childhood, bringing about the union of two long-established rural families. And once he'd had her—he had always been mad about her—he had set about making their lifestyle a whirl of pleasure up until his untimely death.

From time to time she had consoled herself with the thought that perhaps Martyn, as he matured, would cease taking up endless defensive positions against his highly effective father, Gordon, come to recognise his family responsibilities and then pursue them with some skill and determination.

Sadly, all her hopes—and Gordon Prescott's—had been killed off one by one. And she'd had to face some hard facts herself. Hadn't she been left with a legacy of guilt? She had never loved Martyn. Bonded to him from earliest childhood, she had always regarded him with great affection. But *romantic* love? Never! The heart wasn't obedient to the expectations of others. She *knew* what romantic love was. She *knew* about passion—dangerous passion and its infinite temptations—but she hadn't steered away from it in the interests of safety. She had totally succumbed.

All these years later her heart still pumped his name. *Rohan.*

She heard her son's voice clearly. He sounded anxious. "Mummy, are you ready? Grandpa wants to leave."

A moment later, Christopher, a strikingly handsome little boy, dressed in a bright blue shirt with mother-of-pearl buttons and grey cargo pants, tore into the room.

"Come on, come on," he urged, holding out his hand to

her. "He's stomping around the hall and going red in the face. That means his blood pressure is going up, doesn't it?"

"Nothing for you to worry about, sweetheart," Charlotte answered calmly. "Grandpa's health is excellent. Stomping is a way to get our attention. Anyway, we're not late," she pointed out.

It had been after Martyn's death, on her father's urging, that she and Christopher had moved into the Lodge. Her father was sad and lonely, finding it hard getting over the big reversals in his life. She knew at some point she *had* to make a life for herself and her son. But where? She couldn't escape the Valley. Christopher loved it here. It was his home. He loved his friends, his school, his beautiful environment and his bond with his grandfather. It made a move away from the Valley extremely difficult, and there were other crucial considerations for a single mother with a young child.

Martyn had left her little money. They had lived with his parents at their huge High Grove estate. They had wanted for nothing, all expenses paid, but Martyn's father—knowing his son's proclivities—had kept his son on a fairly tight leash. His widow, so all members of the Prescott family had come to believe, was undeserving.

"Grandpa runs to a timetable of his own," Christopher was saying, shaking his golden-blond head. She too was blonde, with green eyes. Martyn had been fair as well, with greyish-blue eyes. Christopher's eyes were as brilliant as blue-fire diamonds. "You look lovely in that dress, Mummy," he added, full of love and pride in his beautiful mother. "Please don't be sad today. I just wish I was seventeen instead of seven," he lamented. "I'm just a kid. But I'll grow up and become a great big success. You'll have *me* to look after you."

"My knight in shining armour!" She bent to give him a

big hug, then took his outstretched hand, shaking it back
and forth as if beginning a march. "Onward, Christian
soldiers!"

"What's that?" He looked up at her with interest.

"It's an English hymn," she explained. Her father
wouldn't have included hymns in the curriculum. Her
father wasn't big on hymns. Not since the Tragedy. "It
means we have to go forth and do our best. *Endure*. It was
a favourite hymn of Sir Winston Churchill. You know who
he was?"

"Of course!" Christopher scoffed. "He was the great
English World War II Prime Minister. The country gave
him a *huge* amount of money for his services to the nation,
then they took most of it back in tax. Grandpa told me."

Charlotte laughed. Very well read himself, her father had
taken it upon himself to "educate" Christopher. Christopher
had attended the best school in the Valley for a few years
now, but her father took his grandson's education much further, taking pride and delight it setting streams of general,
historical and geographical questions for which Christopher
had to find the answers. Christopher was already computer
literate but her father wasn't—something that infuriated
him—and insisted he find the answers in the books in the
well-stocked library. Christopher never cheated. He always
came up trumps. Christopher was a very clever little boy.

Like his father.

The garden party was well underway by the time they
finished their stroll along the curving driveway. Riverbend
had never looked more beautiful, Charlotte thought, pierced
by the same sense of loss she knew her father was expe-
riencing—though one would never have known it from
his confident Lord of the Manor bearing. Her father was
a handsome man, but alas not a lot of people in the Valley

liked him. The mansion, since they had moved, had under-
gone very necessary repairs. These days it was superbly
maintained, and staffed by a housekeeper, her husband—a
sort of major-domo—and several ground staff to bring the
once-famous gardens back to their best. A good-looking
young woman came out from Sydney from time to time,
to check on what was being done. Charlotte had met her
once, purely by accident...

The young woman had left her Mercedes parked off the
broad gravelled driveway so she could take a good look
at the Lodge, screened from view by a grove of mature
trees. Charlotte had been deadheading the roses when
her uninvited visitor—brunette, dark-eyed, in a glamorous black power suit worn with a very stylish snow-white
ruffled blouse—had near tumbled into view on her very
high heels.

"Oh, good afternoon! Hope I didn't startle you?" she'd
called, the voice loud and very precise.

Well, sort of, Charlotte thought. "You did rather," she
answered mildly. The woman's greeting had been pleasant enough. The tone wasn't. It was seriously imperative.
Charlotte might as well have been a slack employee who
needed checking up on. "May I help you?" She was aware
she was being treated to a comprehensive appraisal. A
head-to-toe affair.

The young woman staggered a few steps further across
the thick green grass, thoroughly aerating it. She had to
give up as the stiletto heels of her expensive shoes sank
with every step. "I don't think so. I'm Diane Rodgers, by
the way."

"Well, hello, Diane Rodgers," Charlotte said with a
smile.

Ms Rodgers responded to that with a crisp look. "I've
been appointed by the new owner to oversee progress at

Riverbend. I just thought I'd take a look at the Lodge while I was at it."

"May I ask if you're an estate agent?" Charlotte knew perfectly well she wasn't, but she was reacting to the tone.

"Of course I'm not!" Ms Rodgers looked affronted. An estate agent, indeed!

"Just checking. The Lodge is private property, Ms Rodgers. But I'm sure you know that."

"Surely you have no objection to my taking a look?" The question was undisguisedly sarcastic. "I'm not making an inspection, after all."

"Which would be entirely inappropriate," Charlotte countered.

"Excuse me?" Ms Rodgers's arching black brows rose high.

"No offence, Ms Rodgers, but this is *private* property." The woman already knew that and didn't care. Had she tried a friendly approach, things might have gone differently.

As it was, Diane Rodgers was clearly on a power trip.

She gave an incredulous laugh, accompanied by a toss of her glossy head. "No need to get on your high horse. Though I expect it's understandable. You couldn't bear to part with the place. Isn't that right? You're the daughter of the previous owner." It was a statement, not a question.

"Why would you assume that?" Charlotte resumed deadheading the exquisite deep crimson Ecstasy roses.

"I've *heard* about you, Mrs Prescott." The emphasis was heavy, the smile *knowing*—as if Charlotte's secret was out. She had spent time in an institution. Possibly mental. "You're every bit as beautiful as I've been told."

"Beauty isn't the be all and end all. There are more important things. But may I ask who told you that?" There was a glint in Charlotte's crystal-clear green eyes.

"Sorry, that would be telling. You know yourself how

people love to talk. But being rich and beautiful can't prevent tragedy from occurring, can it? I hear you lost a brother when you were both children. Then a husband only a while back. Must have been frightful experiences? Both?"

Charlotte felt her stomach lurch. Who had this remarkably insensitive young woman spoken to? Someone she'd met in the village? Nicole, Martyn's younger sister? Nicole had always resented her. If Ms Rodgers's informant *had* been Nicole she would have learned a lot—most of it laced with vitriol.

A moment passed. "I'm sure you heard about that too, Ms Rodgers," Charlotte said quietly. "Now, you must excuse me. I have things to do. Preparations for dinner, for one."

"Just your father and your son, I'm told?"

It was more or less a taunt, and it bewildered Charlotte. Why the aggression? The expression on Ms Rodgers's face was hardly compassionate. Charlotte felt a wave of anger flow over her. "I must go in, Ms Rodgers." She folded her secateurs, then placed them in the white wicker basket at her feet. "Do please remember in future the Lodge is off-limits."

Diane Rodgers had intended to sound coolly amused, but she couldn't for the life of her disguise her resentment—which happened to be extreme. Who *was* this Charlotte Prescott to be so hoity-toity? She had well and truly fallen off her pedestal. At least that was the word. "Suit yourself!" she clipped, making too swift an about turn. She staggered, and had to throw a balancing arm aloft, making for the safety of solid ground.

Everyone appeared to be dressed to the nines for the Open Day. Filmy pastel dresses and pretty wide-brimmed hats were all the rage. Women had learned to take shelter from

the blazing Australian sun. Sunscreen. Hats. Charlotte re-
called how her mother had always looked after her skin,
making sure her daughter did the same. Early days. These
days her mother didn't talk to her often. Her mother didn't
talk to *anyone* from the old days. Certainly not her ex-
husband. Her parents had divorced two years after the
Tragedy. Her mother had remarried a few years after that,
and lived in some splendour in Melbourne's elite Toorak.
If she had ever hoped her mother would find solace in her
beautiful grandson, Christopher, she had been doomed to
bitter disappointment. There had only been *one* boy in her
mother's life: her pride and joy, her son Matthew.

"Mummy, can I please go off with Peter?" Christopher
jolted her out of her sad thoughts. Peter Stafford was
Christopher's best friend from day one at pre-school. He
stood at Christopher's shoulder with a big grin planted on
his engaging little face.

"I don't see why not." Charlotte smiled back. "Hello
there, Peter. You're looking very smart." She touched a
hand to his checked-cotton clad shoulder.

"Am I?" Peter blushed with pleasure, looking down at
his new clothes. Christopher had told him in advance he
was wearing long trousers, so Peter had insisted his mother
buy him a pair. His first. He felt very grown-up.

Christopher hit him mildly in the ribs. "You know
Mummy's only being nice."

"I *mean* it, Peter." Charlotte glanced over Peter's head.
"Mum and Dad are here?"

Peter nodded. "Angie too." Angie was his older sister.
"We had to wait ages for Angie to change her dress. I liked
the first dress better. Then she had to fix her hair again.
She was making Mum really angry."

"Well, I'm sure everyone has settled down," Charlotte
offered soothingly. She knew Angela Stafford—as difficult

a child as Peter was trouble-free. "We're all here to enjoy ourselves, and it's a beautiful day." Charlotte placed a loving hand on top of her son's head. "Check in with me from time to time, sweetheart?"

"Of course." He smiled up at her, searching her face in a near-adult way. "If you prefer, Pete and I can stay with you."

"Don't be silly!" she scoffed. "Off you go." Christopher— her little man!

The boys had begun to move away when Peter turned back. "I'm very sorry Riverbend is going out of the family, Mrs Prescott," he said, his brown eyes sweetly sympathetic. "Sorry for you *and* Mr Marsdon. Riverbend would have come to Chris."

Charlotte almost burst into tears. "Well, you know what they say, Peter," she managed lightly. "All good things must come to an end. But thank you. You're a good boy. A credit to your family."

"If *he* is, so am I!" Christopher crowed, impatiently brushing his thick floppy golden hair off his forehead. It was a gesture Charlotte knew well.

She turned her head away. She had to keep her spirits up. Her father was deeply involved in a conversation with the rotund, flush-faced Mayor. The Mayor appeared to be paying careful attention. The Marsdon name still carried a lot of clout. She walked on, waving a hand to those in the crowd who had stuck by her and her father.

Her parents' separation, and subsequent divorce, had split the Valley. Her beautiful, very dignified mother had chaired most of the Valley's charity functions, opening up the grounds of Riverbend for events much like today's. She had been well respected. Her father had never approached that high level of Valley approval, though he was supremely unaware of it such was his unshakeable self-confidence.

The Tragedy had torn her mother to pieces. Her father, grief-stricken, had managed to survive.

What exactly had happened to *her*? She had grown up knowing her mother loved her, but that Matthew, her older brother, the firstborn, was the apple of their mother's eye— her favourite. Her mother was the sort of woman who doted on a *son*. Charlotte hadn't minded at all. She had adored her brother too. Matthew had been a miraculously happy boy. A child of light. And he'd always had Rohan for his best friend. Rohan had been the young son of a single mother in the Valley—Mary Rose Costello.

Mary Rose, orphaned at an early age, had been "raised right" by her maternal grandmother, a strict woman of modest means, who had sent her very pretty granddaughter to the district's excellent convent school. Mary Rose Costello, with the Celt's white skin and red hair, had been regarded by the whole community as a "good girl". One who didn't "play around". Yet Mary Rose Costello, too young to be wise, had blotted her copybook by falling pregnant. Horror of horrors out of wedlock or even an engagement. The odd thing was, in that closely knit Valley, no one had been able to come up with the identity of Rohan's father. Lord knew they had all speculated, long and hard.

Mary Rose had never confided in anyone—including her bitterly shocked and disappointed grandmother. Mary Rose had never spoken the name of her child's father, but everyone was in agreement that he must have been a stunningly handsome man. And clever. Rohan Costello, born on the wrong side of the blanket, was far and away the handsomest, cleverest boy in the Valley. When Mary Rose's grandmother had died, she'd had the heart to leave her granddaughter and her little son the cottage. Mary Rose had then worked as a domestic in both the Marsdon and Prescott residences. She'd also done dressmaking. She had, in fact, been a very fine dressmaker, with natural skills. It was Charlotte's mother who had encouraged Mary Rose to take in orders, spreading the word to her friends across the Valley. So the Costellos had survived, given her mother's continuing patronage.

Up until the Tragedy.

People were milling about on the lush open lawn that stretched a goodly distance to all points of the compass, or taking shelter from the sun beneath the magnolia trees, heavy with plate-sized waxy cream flowers. Children were playing hide and seek amid the hedges; others romped on the grass. The naughty ones were running under the spray from the playing fountain until some adult stopped them before they got soaked. Everyone looked delighted to have been invited. A huge white marquee had been erected, serving delicious little crustless sandwiches, an amazing variety of beautifully decorated cupcakes, and lashings of strawberries and cream. White wine, a selection of fruit juices and the ubiquitous colas and soft drinks were also provided. No one would be allowed to get sozzled on alcohol that afternoon.

Charlotte had a few pleasant words with dozens of people as she threaded her way through the crowd. Her smile was starting to feel like a glaze on her face. It wasn't easy, appearing relaxed and composed, given the melancholy depths of her feelings, but she'd had plenty of practice. Years of containing her grief had taught control, if nothing else. Years of going down to breakfast with the Prescotts, a smile glued to her face, after another fierce encounter with Martyn. At such times he had hit her. Lashed out. Nowhere it would show. That would have caused an uproar. Though spoilt rotten by his mother and sister, his father would swiftly have taken him to account. Domestic violence was totally unacceptable. A man *never* hit a woman. It was unthinkable. Cowardly.

Only Martyn, who had turned out to be a bully, had desperately wanted what she could never give him. Her undivided love. He had even been jealous of Christopher. Had he ever dared lift a hand to her son she would have left him. But as it was, pride had held her in place. It wasn't as though she could have rung home and said, *I'm up to the neck with this marriage. I want out. I'm coming home.*

Her mother had been endeavouring to make a new life for herself elsewhere. Her father at that stage would have told her to "pull her socks up" and make her marriage work. It was only after Martyn had been killed and the scandalous circumstances were on public record that her father had welcomed her back—lonely, and totally unused to running a house. That was women's work. He'd detested the cleaning ladies who came in from time to time. His daughter would take over and cook him some decent meals. Such was his Lord of the Manor mentality. Besides, he loved his little grandson. "Chip off the old block!" he used to say, when Christopher unquestionably *wasn't*.

He took it for granted that Charlotte would stay, when she knew she could not. But when would the right time arrive? Christopher was now seven. No longer a small child.

Everyone was agog to meet the new mystery owner. So far he hadn't appeared, but an hour into the afternoon a helicopter suddenly flew overhead, disappearing over the roof of the mansion to land on the great spread of lawn at the rear of the house. Ten minutes later there was a little fanfare that got everyone's attention. A tall man, immaculately tailored with a red rosebud in his lapel, followed by no less a personage than Ms Diane Rodgers in full garden party regalia, came through the front door.

Even at a distance one could see this was someone quite out of the ordinary. He moved with lithe grace across the colonnaded verandah, coming to stand at the top of the short flight of stone stairs that led to the garden. His eyes surveyed the smiling crowd as he lifted a hand.

Immediately, enthusiastic clapping broke out. Here was their host at last! And didn't he look the part! They were just so thrilled—especially the children, who had stared up in wonderment at the big silver helicopter with its loud whirring rotors.

How is Dad going to handle this? Charlotte thought.

Her father revealed his class. He strolled out of the crowd, perhaps with a certain swagger, to greet the CEO of the company that had bought the ancestral home. "Come along, Charlotte," he commanded, as he drew alongside her. "It's just you and me now. Time to greet the new owner. I very much suspect he's more than just a CEO."

Unfailingly, Charlotte supported her father.

"My, he *is* a handsome man." Her father pitched his voice low. "And a whole lot younger than I would have expected," he tacked on in some surprise. "I fully antici-pated someone in their late forties at least. Hang on—don't I know him?"

Charlotte couldn't say whether he did or he didn't. Even with the broad brim of her picture hat the slanting sun was in her eyes. But she did manage to put a lovely welcoming smile on her face. They were on show. Anyone who was anyone in the Valley was ranged behind them—every last man, woman and child keen observers of this meeting. This was an historic day. The Marsdons, for so long lords and ladies of the Valley, now displaced, were expected to act with grace and aplomb.

Except it didn't happen that way.

"Good God, Costello—it *can't* be you?" Vivian Randall bellowed like an enraged bull.

He came to such an abrupt halt Charlotte, slightly behind him, all but slammed into him, clutching at his arm to steady herself. She saw the blood draining out of her father's face. A hard man to surprise, he looked utterly pole-axed.

She, herself, had felt no portent of disaster. No inkling that another great turning point in her life had arrived. She couldn't change direction. She was stuck in place, with such a tangle of emotions knotted inside her they could never be untied.

There wasn't a flicker of answering emotion on the man's striking, highly intelligent face. "Good afternoon, Mr Marsdon," he said suavely, coming down the stone steps to greet them. Effortless charm. An overlay of natural command. His voice was cultured, the timbre dark. An extremely attractive voice. One people would always listen to. "Charlotte." He turned his head to look at her. Blazing blue eyes consumed her, the electric *blueness* in startling contrast to his colouring—crow-black hair and brows, olive skin that was tanned to a polished bronze. The searing gaze remained fixed on her.

She was swamped by an overwhelming sense of unreality.

Rohan!

The intervening years were as nothing—carried away as if by a king tide. The day of reckoning had come. Hadn't she always known it would? Her heart was pumping double time. The shock was devastating—too excruciating to be borne. She had thought she had built up many protective layers. Now she was blown away by her own emotional fragility. She tried to get her breath, slow her palpitating heart. She felt as weak as a kitten. She raised one trembling hand to her temple as a great stillness started to descend on her. She was vaguely aware she was slipping sideways...

No, no—don't give way! Hold up!

"Rohan!" she breathed.

He was as familiar to her as she was to herself. Yet he had never given a hint of warning—right up until this very day. It was cruel. Rohan had never been cruel. But it was abundantly clear he wanted to shock her far more than he wanted to shock her father. He wanted to stun *her* to her very soul. She read it in his dynamic face. Revenge, smoothly masked. But not to her. She knew him too well. So long as there was memory, the past lived on. One might long to forget, but memory wouldn't allow it.

Her pride broke.

"You do *this* to me, Rohan?" She knew she sounded pitiful. The immediate world had turned from radiant sunshine to a swirling grey fog. It smothered her like a thick blanket. Her ears seemed stuffed with cotton wool. She was moving beyond complete awareness, deeper into the fog, oblivious to the strong arms that shot out with alacrity to gather her up.

A little golden-haired boy ran out of the crowd, crying over and over in a panic, "Mummy...Mummy... Mummy!"

His grandfather, beside himself with sick rage, tried to catch him. The boy broke away, intent on only one thing: following the tall stranger who was carrying his beautiful mother back into the house.

This was the new owner of Riverbend! By now everyone was saying his name, turning one to the other, themselves in a state of shock.

Rohan Costello.

Fate had a way of catching up with everyone.

CHAPTER TWO

Silver Valley, summer fourteen years ago

IT WAS one of those endless afternoons of high summer—glorious months of the school vacation, when the heat sent them racing from the turquoise swimming pool in the mansion's grounds into the river. It meandered through the valley and lay in a broad glittering curve at Riverbend's feet. They knew they were supposed to keep to the pool that afternoon, but it wasn't as though they weren't allowed to take frequent dips in the river. After all, their father had had a carpenter erect a diving dock for their pleasure. Prior to that they had used a rope and an old tyre, fixed to stout branches of a river gum to swing from.

She was twelve, and very much part of the Pack of Four, as they had become known throughout the Valley. She didn't feel honoured to be allowed to tag along with the boys. She *was* one of them. All three boys were inseparable friends: her older brother Mattie, Rohan—Mrs Costello's son—a courtesy title insisted on by their mother, because Mrs Costello was really a miss, but who cared?—and Martyn Prescott, young son of the neighbouring estate, High Grove. Charlotte was their muse.

Although she would have died rather than say it aloud, Rohan was her shining white knight. She loved him. She loved the burning blue looks he bent on her. But these days a kind of humming tension had cut into their easy affection. Once or twice she'd had the crazy desire to kiss him. Proof, if any were needed, that she was fast growing up.

Rohan easily beat them into the water that day, striking out into the middle of the stream, the ripples on the dark green surface edged with sparkles the sunlight had cast on the river. "What's keeping you?" he yelled, throwing a long tanned arm above water. "Come on, Charlie. You can beat the both of them!"

He was absolutely splendid, Rohan! Even as a boy he had a glamour about him. As her mother had once commented, "Rohan's an extraordinary boy—a born leader, and so good for my darling Mattie!" In those early days their mother had been very protective of her only son.

"Won't do him a bit of good, wrapping him in cotton wool." That irritated comment always came from their father, who was sure such mollycoddling was holding his son back.

Perhaps he was right? But their mother took no notice. Unlike her young daughter, who enjoyed splendid health, Matthew had suffered from asthma since infancy. Mattie's paediatrician had told their anxiety-ridden mother he would most likely grow out of it by age fourteen. It was that kind of asthma.

That fatal day Charlotte remembered running to the diving dock, her long, silver-blonde hair flying around her face. It was Martyn who had pulled her hair out of its thick plait. It was something he loved to do. Most of the time she rounded on him—"How stupid, Martyn!" was her usual protest as she began to re-plait it.

"You look better that way, Charlie. One day you're going to be an absolute knockout. Mum and Dad say that. Not

Nicole, of course. She's as jealous as hell. One day we're going to get married. Mum says that too."

"Dream on!" she always scoffed. Get married, indeed! Some husband Martyn would make.

Mattie always laughed, "Boy, has he got a crush on you, Charlie!"

She chose not to believe it. She didn't know then that some crushes get very crushed.

Rohan never laughed. Never joked about it. He kept silent on that score. The Marsdons and the Prescotts were the privileged children of the Valley. Certainly not Rohan Costello, who lived with his mother on the outskirts of town in a little cottage hardly big enough to swing a cat. Their mother said the pair would have to shift soon.

"Rohan is quickly turning into a man!"

At fourteen, nearing fifteen, it was apparent the fast-growing Rohan would easily attain six feet and more in maturity. Mattie, on the other hand, was small for his age. Rohan was by far the strongest and the best swimmer, though she was pretty good herself—but built for speed rather than endurance.

Totally unselfconscious, even with her budding breasts showing through her swimsuit and her long light limbs gleaming a pale gold, with Rohan—her hero—watching, she made a full racing dive into the water, striking out towards him as he urged her on, both of them utterly carefree, not knowing then that this was the last day they would ever swim in the river.

Years later she would shudder when she remembered their odd near-total absorption in one another that summer afternoon. A boy and a girl. One almost fifteen, the other twelve.

Romeo and Juliet.

Martyn appeared angry with them, sniping away. Jealous. Mattie was his normal sweet self. At one stage he called out that he was going to swim across to the opposite bank, where beautiful weeping willows bent their branches towards the stream.

"Stay with us, Mattie," Rohan yelled, cupping his hands around his mouth.

"What's the matter? Reckon I can't do it?" Mattie called back, sounding very much as if he was going to take up the challenge.

"'Course you can!" she had shouted, always mindful of her brother's self-esteem, undermined by his sickness. "But do like Rohan says, Mattie. Stay with us."

Mattie appeared persuaded. He turned in their direction, only then Martyn yelled, his voice loud with taunt, "Don't be such a cream puff, Marsdon! Are you always going to do what Mummy says? Are you always going to stick by Rohan's side? Rohan will look after Mummy's little darling. Isn't that his job? Go for it, Mattie! Don't be such a wimp!"

"Shut up, Martyn!" Rohan roared, in a voice none of them had ever heard before. It was an adult voice. The voice of command.

Immediately Martyn ceased his taunts, but Mattie confounded them all by kicking out towards the opposite bank, his thin arms stiff and straight in the water.

"Perhaps we should let him?" Charlotte had appealed to Rohan, brows knotted. "Mummy really does mollycoddle him."

"You can say that again!" Martyn chortled unkindly. Everyone in the Valley knew how protective Barbara Marsdon was of her only son.

"I'm going after him." It only took a little while of watching Mattie's efforts for Rohan to make the decision. "You shouldn't have taunted him, Martyn. You're supposed to be Mattie's friend. He's trying to be brave, but the brave way is the safest way. Mattie doesn't have your strength, or mine. He isn't the strongest of swimmers."

"He'll make it." Martyn was trying not to sound anxious, but his warier brain cells had kicked in. Rohan was right. He shouldn't have egged Mattie on. He went to say something in his own defence, only Rohan had struck out in his powerful freestyle while Charlotte followed.

Martyn chose to remain behind. He thought they were both overreacting. Mattie would be okay. Sure he would! The distance between the banks at that point wasn't all that wide. The water was warm. The surface was still. There was no appreciable undercurrent. Well, not really. The waters were much murkier on the other side, with the wild tangle of undergrowth, the heavy overhang of trees, the resultant debris that would have found its way into the river. For someone like Rohan the swim would be no more than a couple of lengths of the pool. But for Mattie?

Hell, they could be in the middle of a crisis, Martyn realised—too late.

One minute Mattie's thin arms were making silver splashes in the water, and then to their utter horror his head, gilded by sunlight, disappeared beneath the water.

All of a sudden the river that had taken them so many times into its wonderful cool embrace seemed a frightening place.

"Oh, God—oh, God!" Charlotte shrieked, knowing in her bones something was wrong. "Get him, Rohan!" she cried hysterically.

"Come on, don't be stupid, Charlie. He's only showing off," Martyn shouted at her, starting to feel desperately worried. The traumas of childhood had a way of echoing down the years. Martyn felt shivers of prescience shoot into his gut.

Charlotte ignored him, heart in her mouth. Martyn never was much good in a crisis. It was Rohan who knifed through the dark green water with the speed of a torpedo.

She went after him, showing her own unprecedented burst of speed. "God—oh, God!" Tears were pouring down her face, lost in river water.

There was no sign of Matthew. She knew he wouldn't be playing games. Matthew was enormously considerate of others. He would never frighten her, never cause concern to the people he loved. He loved her. He loved Rohan, his best friend. He wouldn't even have caused dread to Martyn, who had taunted him either.

"Mattie…Mattie *Mattie…!*" She was yelling his name at the top of her lungs, startling birds that took off in a kaleidoscope of colour.

Rohan too had disappeared, diving beneath the dark green water. She followed his example, fear reverberating deep within her body. Lungs tortured, she had to surface for air. As she came up she thought she saw something shimmering—a *shape* moving downstream. She went after it. Rohan beat her to it. She was screaming in earnest now. Rohan was cradling a clearly unconscious Mattie like a baby, holding him out of the water in his strong arms. A thin runnel of blood was streaming off Mattie's pale temple.

Fate could swoop like an eagle from a clear blue sky.

"I'll tow him to the bank," Rohan shouted to her. His voice was choked, his handsome young face twisted in terror. 'I'll try CPR. Keep at it. Charlie—get help."

But Mattie was gone. She *knew* it. Lovely, laughing Mattie. The best brother in the world.

A swim across the river. She could have done it easily. Yet Mattie might have plunged into a deep sea in the blackness of night. There was no sign of Martyn either. He must have run back to the house for help. She thought she might as well drown herself with Mattie gone. There would be no life at Riverbend now. Her mother would most likely go mad. She knew her father would somehow survive. But her mother, even if she could get through the years of annihilating grief, wouldn't stay within sight of the river where her adored Matthew had drowned. She would go away, leaving Charlotte and her father alone.

Except for the gentle shadow of Matthew Marsdon, who would always be fourteen.

The whole tragic thing would be blamed on someone. Her inner voice gave her the sacrificial name.

Rohan.

Rohan the born leader, who would be judged by her parents, the Prescotts, and a few others in the Valley resentful of the Costello boy's superior looks and high intelligence over their own sons, to have let Matthew Marsdon drown.

Such an intolerable burden to place on the shoulders of a mere boy. A crime, and Rohan Costello was innocent of the charge.

The present. The garden party.

Rohan Costello had returned to the scene of his childhood devastation. That showed passion and courage. It also showed that the cleverest boy in the Valley had become extraordinarily successful in life. Matthew Marsdon's tragic death had locked the daughter, Charlotte, and Costello even more closely together. Eventually they'd gone beyond the boundaries, but that had never been known, or if suspected never proved. What *was* known was that the Tragedy had never driven them apart—even when Charlotte's parents, in particular her mother Barbara, had burned with something approaching hatred for the boy she had in a way helped nurture.

There had only been one course left to the Costellos. Mother and son had been virtually driven out of the Valley, the sheer weight of condemnation too great.

The brutality of it!

People could only wonder if Rohan Costello had returned to Silver Valley to settle old scores? The past was never as far away as people liked to pretend.

Charlotte's faint lasted only seconds, but when she was out of it and the world had stopped spinning she was still in a state of shock, her body trembling with nerves. She was lying on one of the long sofas in the drawing room, her head and her feet resting on a pile of silk cushions. Her hair had all but fallen out of its elegant arrangement. She was minus her hat and, she noted dazedly, her expensive sandals.

Rohan was at her head. Christopher was at her feet. Diane Rodgers and a couple of her mother's old friends stood close by. Her mother's friends' watching faces were showing their concern. Not so Ms Rodgers, whose almond eyes were narrow. There was no sign of her father, but George Morrissey, their family doctor, hurried in, calling as he came, "Charlie, dear, whatever happened?"

Morrissey had brought the Marsdon children into the world, and Charlotte had always been a great favourite.

"How are you feeling now?" He sat down beside her to take her pulse. A few more checks, and then, satisfied there was nothing serious about the faint, he raised her up gently, while Rohan Costello, the new owner, resettled the cushions as a prop at her back.

"The heat, George," she explained, not daring to look up at Rohan, who had so stunningly re-entered her life. What she wanted to do was seize hold of her little son and run for her life. Except there was no escape. Not now. "I must be going soft."

"That'll be the day!" the doctor scoffed.

"Mummy?" Christopher's lovely olive skin had turned paper-white. "Are you all right?"

"I'm fine, darling." She held out a reassuring hand. "Come here to me." She tried hard to inject brightness into her voice. "I love you, Chrissie."

"Mummy, I love you too. You've never fainted before." He clutched her hand, staring anxiously into her face.

"I'm fine now, sweetheart. Just a little dizzy." She drew him down onto the spot Dr Morrissey had readily vacated, putting a soothing arm around him and dropping a kiss on the top of his golden head. "I'll get up in a minute."

"Give it a little longer, Charlie," Morrissey advised, happy to see her natural colour returning. He very much suspected extreme shock was the cause of Charlotte's faint. Incredible to think young Costello had become so successful. Then again, not. Rohan Costello *had* been an exceptionally bright lad.

"This *is* a surprise, Rohan," he said, turning to hold out his hand.

Rohan Costello took it in a firm grip. The doctor could hardly say, given the circumstances of Rohan Costello's departure, *Welcome back to Silver Valley*!

"It's good to see you again, Dr Morrissey," Rohan answered smoothly. "You were always kind to my mother and me."

"You were both very easy to be kind to, Rohan," Morrissey assured him with genuine warmth. "And how is your mother?"

"She's doing very well, sir," Rohan responded pleasantly, but it was obvious he wasn't going to be more forthcoming.

"Good, good! I'm very glad to hear it. Do you intend to spend much time in the Valley, Rohan?" Morrissey dared to ask. "You must have become a very successful businessman?"

Rohan gave him a half smile that bracketed his handsome mouth. "I've had a few lucky breaks, Doctor."

"I think it would have more to do with brain power. You were always very clever."

George Morrissey, the keeper of many secrets, turned back to take another look at Charlotte and her precious boy. What a beautiful child Christopher was, with those glorious blue eyes! One rarely saw that depth of colour. He had delivered Christopher Prescott, Charlotte's baby, who had come a little early. He was sure everyone had believed him. He was the most respected medical doctor in the Valley. After the tragic death of Charlotte's young brother Matthew, and the flight of her mother from the "haunted" Valley, he had become very protective of Charlotte Marsdon, who had gone on to marry a young man who in his opinion had simply not been worthy of her. Martyn Prescott—who himself had met a tragic fate.

Christopher too wanted to talk to the tall stranger—the man who had carried his mother so effortlessly into their house. Well, *his* house now. And it seemed to suit him just fine. Christopher was very thankful the *right* person would have ownership of Riverbend. He looked just the sort of man to look after it.

Christopher stood up, wondering why his mother was trying to grab hold of his arm. He held out his hand, as he had been taught. "Hello, I'm Christopher. We used to live here."

"I know that, Christopher," the man answered quietly, moving in closer.

The man's blue eyes made contact with his own, and Christopher felt transfixed. "Do you know Mummy?" He didn't see how the man could, yet those vibes he seemed to have inherited from someone told him this man and his mother knew one another well. It was a mystery, but there it was!

Charlotte put her feet to the floor, unsure if she could even stand, still not looking at Rohan but acutely aware that the full force of his attention was focused on her and her son. "Mr Costello is a very busy man, Chris," she said. Christopher was so sharp. "We mustn't keep him from mingling with his guests."

"No, Mummy." Christopher nodded his head in agreement, but continued with a further question. "*How* do you know my mother?" It seemed important he find out. Perceptive beyond his years, he felt the tension between his mother and the tall stranger. He couldn't figure it out. But it was *there*. Mummy was nice to everyone, yet she wasn't being exactly nice to Mr Costello. Something had to be worrying her.

"Your mother and I grew up together, Christopher," Rohan explained. "I left the Valley when I was seventeen. I'm Rohan. No need to call me Mr Costello."

"Oh, I'd like that," Christopher said, his cheeks taking on a gratified flush. "We thought you were going to be pretty old. But you're *young*!"

"Your mother has never mentioned me?"

Christopher shook his blond head. "Did you know my dad died?" He edged closer to the man. It was like being drawn by a magnet. It sort of *thrilled* him. He felt he could follow this man Rohan like the disciples in Bible stories had followed their Master. It both pleased and puzzled him.

"Yes, I did, Christopher. I'm very sorry." Rohan's voice was gentle, yet his expression was stern.

"There's just Mummy and me now." Christopher felt the sting of tears at the back of his eyes. He had loved his dad. Of course he had. One *had* to love one's dad. But never like he loved his mother. What was really strange was that he cared for his grumpy old grandfather more than he had cared for his dad. "And Grandpa, of course," he tacked on. "You must have known my dad and Uncle Mattie?"

"Oh, darling, not all these questions!" Charlotte spoke with agitation. He had sussed out enough already. Something had happened to Christopher of late. He was picking up on vibes, on looks and words that appeared to him laden with meaning. He was growing up too fast.

For once, Christopher didn't heed her. "Uncle Mattie is still around," he told Rohan, staring up at him. He was really surprised by the way he felt drawn to his man. "I often *feel* Uncle Mattie around."

Rohan didn't laugh or deride his claim. "I believe it, Christopher," he said. "I feel Mattie too, at different times. He would have *loved* you."

"Would he?" Christopher was immensely pleased. Uncle Mattie would have loved him! He was liking Rohan more and more. "Mummy said I looked like him when I was little." He continued to meet Rohan's amazing blue eyes. They glittered like jewels. "Do I?"

Rohan considered that carefully. "You might have, Christopher, when you were younger. But not now."

"No." Christopher shook his blond head, as though his own opinion had been confirmed. "I don't look like anyone, really," he confided.

Oh, yes, you do!

Charlotte kept her head down, her heart fluttering wildly in her breast. Christopher's face had changed as the baby

softness had firmed and his features became more pronounced. Heredity. It was all so *dangerous*.

It was Diane Rodgers who located Charlotte's expensive
sandals, then passed them to her in such a manner as to
suggest a hurry-up. There was a faint accompanying glare
as well. Charlotte bent to put her strappy sandals back on,
then made an attempt to fix her hair. She felt totally dis-
orientated. And there was Christopher, chattering away to
Rohan as if he had known him all his young life. It almost
broke her.

"Here's your hat, love." A familiar face swam into view.
Kathy Nolan—a good friend to her mother and a good
friend to her. "It's beautiful."

"Thank you, Kathy." Charlotte took the picture hat in
her hand.

"Feeling better now, love?" Kathy Nolan was very fond
of Charlotte.

"Much better, thank you, Kathy. I'm so sorry I embarrassed you all. The heat got to me."

Kathy, a kindly woman, let that go. A beautiful breeze
was keeping the temperature positively balmy. Charlotte
had fainted because Rohan Costello was the last man in
the universe she would have expected to buy the Marsdon
mansion, Kathy reckoned. To tell the truth she felt a little
freaked out herself. Rohan Costello, of all people! And
didn't he look *marvellous*! Always a handsome boy, the
adult Rohan took her breath away. Many people in the
Valley—herself and her husband certainly—had been unhappy when the Costellos had left after Rohan had completed his final year at secondary school. Later they had
learned he was their top achiever. The highest category.
No surprise.

Poor Barbara had never made allowances for the ages

of the other children when Mattie had drowned. It had
been a terrible accident. With all the care in the world,
accidents still happened. Yet Barbara had gone on a bitter,
never-ending attack. So very sad! Loss took people in different ways. Bereft of her son, Barbara Marsdon had been
in despair. That inner devastation had brought about the
divorce. The marriage had been beyond repair. Barbara had
told her she'd doubted her ability to be a good mother to
Charlotte. She wasn't functioning properly. That had been
true enough. Charlotte was to remain with her father.

Yet here was Rohan Costello, back in the Valley. Not
only that, taking possession of Riverbend. Fact is far
stranger than fiction, Kathy thought.

Diane Rodgers, looking very glamorous in classic white,
with a striking black and white creation on her head, spoke
up. "Would you like me to help you back to the Lodge, Mrs
Prescott? No trouble, I assure you."

At the sound of those precise tones, Christopher swung
back. "Mummy has *me*," he said, not rudely—he knew
better than that—but he didn't like the way the lady was
speaking to his mother. It didn't sound gentle and caring,
like Mrs Nolan. It sounded more like teachers at his school
when the kids weren't on their best behaviour.

"Wouldn't you like to stay on, Christopher?" Rohan
suggested. "I'm sure you have a friend with you. I'll run
your mother home."

Christopher considered that for a full minute. "I won't
stay if you don't feel well, Mummy," he said, his protective
attitude on show. "Peter will be okay."

Charlotte rose to her feet, hoping she didn't look as desperate as she felt. "Sweetheart, I don't want you to bother
about me. I don't want *anyone* to bother about me. I'm
fine."

"You're sure of that, Charlie?" Morrissey laid a gentle hand on her shoulder.

"You mustn't let me keep you, George." Charlotte gave him a shaky smile. "I know you and Ruth will love wandering around the grounds. They're in tip-top condition."

"That they are!" George Morrissey agreed. He turned back to the tall authoritative figure of the adult Rohan Costello. "I'd be delighted if you'd say hello to my wife, Rohan. She'd love to catch up."

"It would be a pleasure." Rohan gave a slight inclination of his handsome dark head.

The doctor lifted a hand in general farewell, then walked off towards the entrance hall.

"You must allow me to run you back to the Lodge at least, Charlotte," Rohan said, with a compelling undernote she couldn't fail to miss. "I'll make sure Chris gets home."

"Thank you, Rohan," Christopher piped up. "Can't take the helicopter, I suppose?" he joked, executing a full circle, arms outstretched. "Whump, whump, whump!"

"Not that far." Rohan returned the boy's entrancing smile. "But I promise you a ride one day soon."

Christopher looked blown away. "Gee, that's great! Wait until I tell Peter."

"Maybe Peter too," Rohan said.

"That'd be *awesome*! So where's Grandpa?" Christopher suddenly asked of his mother. "Why didn't he come into the house?"

"He may well be outside, Christopher," Rohan answered smoothly. "Why don't you go and see? Your mother is safe with me."

"Is that all right, Mummy? I can go?" Christopher studied her face. His mother was *so* beautiful. The most beautiful mother in the world.

"Of course you can, darling." Charlotte summoned up a smile. "I want you to enjoy yourself."

"Thank you." Christopher shifted his blue gaze back to Rohan. "It's great to meet you, Rohan." He put out his hand. Man to man.

Rohan shook it gravely. "Great to meet you too, Christopher," he responded. *"At long last."*

Many things in life changed. Some things never did.

CHAPTER THREE

THEY were quite alone. It was terrifying. Was she afraid of Rohan? That simply couldn't be. But she was terrified of the emotions that must be raging through him. Terrified of the *steel* in him. Where had her beautiful white knight gone? A shudder ripped through her. This was a Rohan she had never seen.

The village ladies had gone back outside, to enjoy the rest of the afternoon. Diane Rodgers had hovered, but Rohan had given her a taut smile and told her in his dark mellifluous voice to go and take a look at the roses. They were in magnificent full bloom. Ms Rodgers looked as though she had been planning something entirely different. One would have had to be blind to miss Ms Rodgers's keen interest in Rohan. And who could blame her?

The pulverising shock had not worn off. Nor would it for a long time. Now she felt an added trepidation, and—God help her—the old pounding excitement. He looked wonderful. *Wonderful!* The man who had loved her and whom she had loved in return.

Rohan.

She saw how much she still loved him. No one else had ever mattered. But now wasn't the time to fall apart. She had to keep some measure of herself together. "I can walk back to the Lodge," she said, although her voice was reduced to a trembling whisper. "You don't have to take me."

"*Don't* I?"

The slash of his voice cut her heart to ribbons.

God—oh, God!

Recognition of the trouble she was in settled on her.

He took hold of her bare slender arm, pulling her in to his side. "He's *mine*, isn't he?" he ground out. His tone was implacable.

She wasn't up to this. She was a lost soul. She was acutely aware of the pronounced pallor beneath his golden-olive skin. He was in shock too. She wanted to touch his face. Didn't dare. She felt sorrow. Guilt. Pity. Remorse. Her heart was fluttering like a frantic bird in her breast. She had to try to evade the whole momentous issue. She needed time to *think*.

"I don't know what you're talking about, Rohan." She allowed a fallen lock of hair to half-shield her face.

"Is that why you're trembling from head to foot?" he answered curtly. "Christopher is *mine*. My child—not Martyn's."

She tried to disengage herself, but didn't have a hope. He was far too strong. "Are you insane?" Her voice shook with alarm.

"God!" Rohan burst out, his breathing harsh. "Don't play the fool with me, Charlotte. He has *my* eyes. My nose. My mouth. My chin."

Your beautiful smile. The habit you had of flipping your hair back with an impatient hand.

"He's going to get more and more like me," Rohan gritted. "What are you going to do then?"

"Rohan, *please*," she begged, hating herself.

He took no pity on her. It was all he could do not to shake her until her blonde head collapsed against his chest.

Despite himself, he was breathing in the very special scent of her—the freshness, the fragrance. He could breathe her in for ever. He was that much of a fool.

"How could you do this, Charlotte? It's unforgivable what you've done. No *way* is Christopher Martyn's child."

"Please, Rohan, *stop!*" She shut her eyes tight in pain and despair. She was still light-headed.

"You made the decision to banish me from your heart and your head," he accused her. "You know you did. No love in a cottage for Charlotte Marsdon. God, no! Poor Martyn was always crazy about you. You were the ultimate prize, waiting for him. Did he *know* the child wasn't his?"

Years of unhappiness, pain and guilt echoed from her throat. "How *could* he know?" she shouted. "*I* didn't."

"What?" He took a backward glance through the mansion, then led her away into the splendid book-lined library.

Her father had taken his pick of the valuable collection of books. Even in her highly perturbed state she could see their number had been replaced.

"You mean you were having sex with us *both*?" Rohan asked, looking and sounding appalled. "Oh, don't tell me. I don't want to know," he groaned.

She had to turn away from the anger flashing in his blue eyes. "It wasn't like that, Rohan. You were lost to me. Forever lost to me.'

His brief laugh couldn't have been more bitter or disbelieving. "You're lying again. You *knew* I would never let you go. I had to make something of myself, Charlotte. I had to have something to offer you. All I needed was a little time. I told you that. I believed you understood. But, no, you got yourself married to *Martyn* in double-quick time. Poor gutless Martyn, who went around telling everyone who would listen that *I* had goaded Mattie into trying to swim the river. Martyn was the golden boy in the Valley, not me. I was Mary Rose Costello's bastard son. Yet I thought the world would freeze over before *you* ever gave yourself to Martyn."

"Maybe he *took* me, Rohan. Ever think of that?" She threw up her head in a kind of wild defiance, though she was on the verge of breaking down completely.

"What are you *saying*?" There was fire in his eyes.

Rivers of tears were threateningly close. "I don't know *what* I'm saying." Her heart was labouring in her chest. "I never thought I would lay eyes on you again."

"Rubbish!" he responded violently. "You *knew* you would see me again. With Martyn gone. I've given you enough time to recover.'

"There would *never* be enough time." Her green eyes glittered. "What do you expect me to say? Welcome back, Rohan?"

A great anger was running in his veins. Whatever he had expected, it had never been *this*. He had learned early that she and Martyn had had a child—a boy. The agony of it, the pain of loss and betrayal, had nearly driven him mad. Day and night, month after month, year after year he had fought his demons. Charlotte and Martyn. Now he was confronted by the staggering truth. Christopher wasn't Martyn's at all. Christopher was *his*.

How terrible a crime was that? And what about the precautions she was supposed to have taken? "You're a cheat and a liar, Charlotte," he said, low-voiced and dangerous. "And I fully intend to prove it. You told me you loved me. You promised to wait for as long as it took. Why not? We had plenty of time. You were only eighteen. I hadn't even turned twenty-one. *I'm* Christopher's father. Don't look away from me. Don't attempt more lies. I *will* push this further."

"A threat?"

"You bet!" he said harshly, even though to his horror the old hunger was as fierce as ever. Would *nothing* kill it? She was even more beautiful—her beauty more pronounced, more complete. Charlotte who had betrayed him. And herself.

"Please, Rohan, I don't need this now." There was anguish in her face and in her voice. "I can walk back to the Lodge."

"Forget it. I'm driving you. Has your father the faintest clue? Or is he still hiding his head in the sand?" He compelled her out of the comfortable elegance of the library and back into the arched corridor, making for the rear of the house, where a vehicle was garaged and kept for his convenience.

"Dad loves Christopher very much." There was a trembling catch in her voice.

"Not what I asked you," he said grimly.

They were out in the sunshine now. The scent of the white rambling rose that framed the pedimented door and climbed the stone wall filled the air with its lovely nostalgic perfume. More roses rioted in the gardens, and lovely plump peonies—one of her great favourites.

"Chris did have a fleeting look of Mattie for a few years," she offered bleakly. This was the age of DNA. There was no point in trying to delude Rohan. What he said was correct. Christopher would only grow more like him. Hadn't she been buffeted by the winds of panic for some time? "Now that he's lost his little-boy softness the resemblance has disappeared. He has our blond hair."

"Isn't that marvelous?" he exclaimed ironically. "He has the Marsdon blond hair! God knows what might have happened had his hair been crow-black, like mine. Or, even worse, *red* like my mother's."

"I loved you, Rohan." The words flamed out of her.

In response he made a strangled sound of utter disgust. "You must have wept buckets after you decided to drop me. But there's intense satisfaction in my being rich. Daddy turned out to be a real loser with his lack of financial acumen. I had nothing. Too young. Martyn stood to inherit a fortune. Must have ruined your day when you lost him. How come you're living with your father? Didn't Martyn leave you a rich woman?"

"Sad to say, no. It's none of your business, Rohan."

"I beg to differ. It's very much my business. Martyn's father was too smart to let go of the purse strings. And your mother? The self-appointed avenger?"

"My mother has settled—or tried to settle—into a different life. I don't see much of her. She has little interest in my beautiful Chrissie."

"*Our* beautiful Christopher," he corrected curtly, usurping her as the single parent.

"He's not Mattie, you see," she continued sadly. "Really there was no one else for my mother."

Rohan's striking face was set like granite. "She loved you in her way. Of course she did."

"Not enough," she answered simply.

"I think I might find that a blessing," Rohan mused. "Your mother keeping her distance from my son. Your mother is deeply neurotic. She would never accept *me* in any capacity. Not in a hundred lifetimes."

She couldn't deny it. Rohan had been chosen as the scapegoat. She had been the daughter of the family—a girl of twelve. Martyn Prescott the only son of close friends. It had to be Rohan Costello—Mary Rose's boy. "My mother has been steeped in grief, Rohan. Dad has soldiered on."

"Good old Vivian!" Rohan retorted with extreme sarcasm. "The fire's not out in the old boy either. Did you hear the way he bellowed my name?"

Charlotte flinched, defending him quickly. "It was cruel not to let us know."

"Cruel?" Rohan's brilliant eyes shot sparks. "The hide of you to talk of cruelty! I can't believe *your* treachery! I've missed out on the first seven years of my son's life, Charlotte. First words. First steps. Birthdays. The first day at school. How can you possibly make it up to me for that?"

"I can't. I *can't.* I'm so sorry, Rohan. Sorry. Sorry, sorry. Do you want me to go down on my knees? I've raised Christopher as best I could. He's a beautiful, loving, clever child. He's everything in the world to me."

"So that's okay, then, is it? He's everything in the world to *you.* What about *me*? I never held my newborn son in my arms. I was robbed of that great joy. Tell me, how did you manage to put it across Martyn? Or didn't you? It's common knowledge he had a young woman in the car with him. It's a great mercy she wasn't killed or injured as well. Tell me—did he fall out of love with you? Or did he get sick of what little affection you could show him? You didn't love him. Don't tell me you did."

"I married Martyn and what came of it?" she said. "He's dead."

"You weren't responsible for that." He reacted to the pain in her face.

"Wasn't I?"

"So he had a tough time? Why did you do it, Charlotte? The money, the position?"

"I was *pregnant*, Rohan."

"By *me*!" he exploded. "Why didn't you contact me? God knows, I had the right to know."

"I wasn't sure whose child I was carrying, Rohan." Her voice was that of the frightened, isolated young girl she had been.

"Oh, poor, poor you! It couldn't have taken you all that long to find out!"

"Too late," she acknowledged, remembering her shock. "Martyn never did find out. Christopher has changed quite a lot in the past eighteen months."

"I'm not getting this at all," he frowned. "What about the Prescotts?"

"They have their suspicions. Nicole hates me. Always did, I think. We don't see much of them."

"Another plus! So when did you decide to seduce Martyn? I mean have sex with him. Clinch your position in his life."

"I don't want to talk about this, Rohan," she said, in a tight, defensive voice. "It's all over and done with."

"Not by a long shot. I can see you're badly frightened, and you should be. I have every intention of claiming my son."

She stood paralysed. "You can't do that to me."

"Can't I? I *can*, by God!" There was strain and a world of determination in his striking face.

"You can't take him from me, Rohan. You can't mean that. He's my life. I adore him."

"Who would take any notice of *you*? You were supposed to have *adored* me, remember? I don't intend to take our son from you, Charlotte. Unlike you, I do have a heart. *You* are part of the package." He let his eyes rest on her. Beautiful, beautiful, unfaithful Charlotte. "I want you *and* our son. Our boy can't be separated from his mother."

Jets of emotion shot through her. "In the same way you needed to have Riverbend?" she challenged.

"Perhaps I hated to see such a magnificent estate go to

rack and ruin." He shrugged. "I have plans for Riverbend, Charlotte. Plans for the vineyards, a winery, olive groves."

She accepted he had plans without hesitation. "You own the estate—not the company Vortex?"

"I *am* Vortex—and a couple of other affiliated companies as well. And I own Riverbend, lock, stock and barrel. Your father has done virtually nothing in the way of improvements since your grandfather died. I don't particularly dislike your father. I never did. It was your *mother* who was truly horrible to us. You know—your mother—the *great* lady." His eyes glittered with blue light.

"There are big turning points in life, Rohan," she said in a pain-filled voice. "My mother was never the same person after we lost Mattie. Feel pity for her. I do. Mattie's death blasted her apart. God knows how *I* would continue if anything…if anything—" She broke off in deep distress.

"Oh, stop it." He cut her off ruthlessly. "Nothing is going to happen to Christopher."

"God keep him safe. I've loved and protected him. Taken care of him all these years."

His voice carried both anger and confusion. "Martyn—how did he feel? Of course you always could twist him around your little finger."

"I can't talk about Martyn, Rohan." She focused her gaze on the massed beds of Japanese hybrid petunias—white in one, rosy-pink in another.

"You couldn't have let him down worse than you did me," he said bleakly. "He had *no* suspicions?"

She brought her green gaze back to him. Was he aware she was *devouring* his marvellous face, feature by feature, marking the changes, the refinements of maturity. *Rohan. Her Rohan.* "I told you. I can't talk about this."

"Maybe not today, but you will," he insisted. "You saw

Christopher with me, Charlotte. He accepted me on sight. I won't let him go. You either."

She took in his unyielding expression. "You want to punish me?"

"Every day," he admitted with a grim smile. "My perfect captive—my golden Charlotte, Martyn Prescott's *widow*." His tone was quiet, yet it lashed out at her. "Now, there's no need for you to go into a mad panic. I realise we've both had a tremendous shock today. I'll handle this from now on. You don't have to do or say a thing. I'll be making frequent trips in and out of the Valley. Plenty of time to establish a truly poignant renewal of our old romance. The whole Valley knows how close we were at one time. This will be our second chance. Isn't that wonderful? A second chance. I'm certain you'll have the sense to fall into line."

She found the strength to launch her own attack. "It doesn't really look like I have an option. And Diane Rodgers? What about her? Will you keep her on as your mistress?'

His black brows drew together. "Don't be so ridiculous. Diane is a highly efficient PR person. Nothing more."

"Perhaps you should tell *her* that." She stared at him directly—only he didn't appear to be taking on board what she said.

"God, isn't it *good* to be back in Silver Valley?" he enthused with great irony. "Let me return you to Daddy, Charlotte. We'll take the Range Rover. You've got an awful lot to think about, haven't you? Don't worry about *our* son. I'll bring him safely home."

Of course he would. She trusted him. "All I want is Christopher's happiness," she said.

His magnetic smile turned deeply mocking. "I think I can guarantee that. As for *us*—we're just going to have to work very hard at our respective roles."

"You won't say anything to Christopher?" In her agitation she grasped his arm.

He looked down at her elegant, long fingers. "What do you take me for? I won't be telling him our little secret until I'm sure—*we're* sure—he can handle it."

"Thank you, Rohan." She removed her hand—she knew he wanted her to—overcome by relief and gratitude. Rohan had suffered so much as a boy it would have been impossible for him to heap grief on any child, let alone his own son.

It was her own actions that gave her the most pain. What she had done to Rohan was beyond forgiveness. There was little comfort in the knowledge that she had believed at the beginning she was carrying Martyn's child. She had been taking the pill when she and Rohan had been together, that first year at university in Sydney. A necessary precaution against her falling pregnant. They'd both been so young. Rohan had begged her to give him time to make something of himself so he would be in a position to offer marriage. Growing up as he had, with the social stigma of not knowing who his father was, he'd been intent on doing everything just right.

Yet despite that she *had* fallen pregnant. And by Rohan. She had been certain for some years now. It had taken her over-long to realise the contraceptive pill's efficacy could be put in jeopardy if a woman experienced a bout of sickness like a bad stomach upset. That had happened to her around about that time. A chicken roll at a campus picnic. She and a girlfriend had been very sick for twenty-four hours following the picnic. One had to be so careful in the heat. Chicken was about the worst food there was.

As for Martyn! Even now she couldn't bear to think about that night when he had totally lost his head. All these years later she was still left with mental bruising—far

worse than the physical bruising Martyn had left on her unyielding body. The monstrous reality of it was that Martyn,
her friend from earliest childhood, had taken her against
her will. There was a word for it. She studiously avoided
it. But she remembered the way she had thrashed about as
she'd tried to stop him. It had only excited him further—as
though he'd believed she was playing a game. The comfort-
ing arm he had initially offered her had turned swiftly into
the arm that had so easily overpowered her. Afterwards he
had begged for forgiveness in tears, citing that he'd had too
much to drink.

He *had*. But into their marriage he had told her, with
triumph in her eyes, that her pregnancy had been a sure
way of getting her away from Rohan.

*"You know Rohan will never be in a position to reinvent
himself. I mean, he's really poor. It'll always be a long,
hard hike for him to get ahead. Probably twenty years.
What you need is the life you were born to. A guy like me
to lean on."*

How could she have leant on Martyn when he hadn't
even been able to stand up for himself?

It had been the worst possible start to a disastrous marriage that should never have happened. Only in those days
she had been literally terrified of bringing further trauma
to her already traumatised parents. Facts were facts. She'd
been pregnant. Martyn was the father. They'd been too
young, but he'd adored her. In a way she had brought it all
down on herself.

Her father had given them a lavish wedding at Riverbend.
He had spent a fortune. The Prescotts had been over the
moon at that time, with the union of the two families.
She'd been seen, even then, as a steadying influence on
Martyn.

Many times she had thought she would go to her grave

not telling anyone the truth of what had really happened that awful night. She had so trusted Martyn, and he had been obsessed with taking control of her body. What was going to happen now was quite another matter. Rohan was back. Rohan was indisputably in charge. Christopher would not remain very long not knowing who his real father was. Not that much longer and everyone in the Valley would know. Had Christopher inherited Rohan's raven locks instead of the Marsdon blond hair they would know already. Christopher was fast turning into a dead ringer for his father.

Her father stormed into the entrance hall of the Lodge just as she stepped inside the door. Rohan had dropped her off outside. He knew about the side entrance to the Lodge, of course. It had been an excruciating short ride. Both of them utterly silent, yet unbearably aware of each other. She couldn't even find the courage to ask about his mother. Mrs Costello had always been lovely to her. They had embraced in tears the day she and Rohan had left the Valley.

"Not your fault. Never your fault, Charlotte."

Getting herself married to Martyn Prescott was. It had wrecked their friendship. It had wrecked lives.

So there she was, on what was supposed to have been a picture-perfect day, with her heart slashed to ribbons.

"That was Costello, wasn't it?" A great helpless anger seemed to surround Vivian Marsdon like a cloud.

"You know it was, Dad." She moved past him into the living room, sinking dazedly into an armchair. Her father followed her, remaining standing. He would think that gave him the advantage. "No point in working yourself up. It's not going to do a bit of good. And, really, you can't yell at Rohan. Not ever again. You'll get more than you bargained for. We *all* will. The old days are over—the days when you and Mum attacked Rohan and Mrs Costello at every opportunity.'

"That fire-eater!' Vivian Marsdon snorted, his expression tight.

"And good for her!" Charlotte felt her own anger gather. "All Mrs Costello did was defend her son."

"*Miss* Costello, thank you."

"Don't be so sanctimonious! Maybe she was like a tigress defending her young? Good on her! I admired her immensely for taking on my high and mighty parents. She was driven to it. You were both so cruel. Mum was by far the worst."

"Your mother was off her head, Charlie. I mean she was completely out of it. We had lost our only son. What *did* you expect of us?" he asked, his voice a mix of shame and outrage.

"I expected wisdom, Dad. Compassion, understanding. Not a blind allocation of the blame. It was a terrible freak accident. We're not the only family to have lost loved ones in tragic accidents. Families suffer all over the world— the rich and the poor alike. Please sit down, Dad. Better yet, calm down. Can I tell you, not for the first time, it was Martyn who was at fault? It was Martyn who goaded Mattie into swimming the river. Rohan and I called him back. He *was* coming back. But Martyn wanted to wind Mattie up. Throw down a challenge. Rohan went after Mattie, but Mattie wouldn't stop. He was trying to prove something."

Vivian Marsdon recoiled in near horror. "What *is* this?"

"The *truth* of that terrible afternoon, Dad. The truth you and Mum wouldn't listen to. But you surely heard the version Martyn, coward that he was, put about."

"I—don't—believe—you." There was a kind of delirium

in Vivian's deep, cultured voice. "You worshipped young Costello. You would always be on his side. You would lie for him if you had to."

"What does it matter now, Dad? I give up. Let's say the fault lay with Fate." Charlotte put a hand to her pounding head. "You've only ever believed what you wanted to anyway."

Her father panted with outrage. "To think you would malign your late husband! Poor, dead Martyn! You're still looking to clear Costello, of course."

"You're right about that!" she declared. "All those years ago you and Mum turned on us with deaf ears. You had your own agenda. Martyn was a Prescott. Rohan was a nobody. Only that was far from true, wasn't it? Rohan was always destined to be somebody. Even Mum said it when she was still sane. The two of you made him your scapegoat."

Vivian Marsdon's chin quivered with rage. "He was the ringleader of your silly Pack of Four. You were just a girl. Martyn always played the fool. It was Costello who had to pay for his extreme negligence, his lack of supervision."

"How brutally unfair! Mattie, Martyn and Rohan were all of an age. Why should *Rohan* have to pay?"

"Because we'll never get our son back—that's why," her father thundered. "Don't you understand that? Losing Matthew broke up our marriage. Your mother couldn't bear to stay here. She couldn't bear to be with me though I shared her pain."

"Of course you did, Dad, but never to the same degree. Mum will rake over the ashes of that terrible day until she dies. I wonder how Reiner copes? Sometimes he must feel like he's in prison."

Her father slumped down heavily. "Who cares about Reiner? God knows how your mother married the man.

We'll never get Matthew back. I'll never get *her* back. But we have our splendid little Chrissie. Where is he, anyway?" He stared around, suddenly becoming aware his grandson hadn't yet come home.

"Settle down, Dad," Charlotte begged wearily. "He's with Peter. I'm not going to chain him to me, like Mum did with Mattie. Christopher and Peter are sensible boys. They're only down the drive. "

"He should have come home with you, none the less," Vivian maintained.

He was very seriously disturbed by Rohan Costello's shock return to the Valley. And that wasn't the only reason for his sense of anxiety. What was the effect it was going to have on Charlotte? He wasn't such a fool he didn't know Rohan Costello had once been everything in the world to his daughter. Was Rohan Costello's desire *now* for revenge?

"Chris is enjoying himself, Dad. Don't worry about him. And whatever you do," she added with heavy irony, "don't worry about me—the child who survived. Mum told me in one of her black fits of depression she wished *I* had been the one to die."

Vivian had to steady himself by gripping the sides of his high-backed armchair. "She didn't. She *couldn't*." He was sincerely shocked.

"Sorry, Dad. She *did*. She didn't have to say it anyway. We both knew Mattie was the light of Mum's eyes."

"But, Charlie, dear, she loved you." He was shaking his fair head as though he couldn't believe her disclosure.

"Only as long as Mattie was around." Charlotte took the last clip out of her hair and shook its gleaming masses free.

Vivian Marsdon's tanned skin had gone very white. "Well, *I* love you, Charlotte. *You* were my favourite. I loved

Matthew, of course. But you were my little girl—always so clever and bright and full of life. Your mother wrapped poor Matthew in cotton wool. It was a big mistake, but Barbara would never listen to me."

"She listened to no one when it came to Mattie. It was Rohan who encouraged Mattie to be more outgoing. And look where it got him."

Her father flinched. "It will be impossible to make peace with Costello. Too much history, Charlotte," he said. "I'm tormented by the past. Only the young can spring back from tragedy."

She exhaled a long breath. "If you *can't* make peace, Dad, you will have to learn to be civil. We're going to be seeing a lot of Rohan. He's staying in the Valley for some time."

"So what did he say?"

"That he's going to make Riverbend, its vineyards and the olive groves, the best in the Valley. He's going to produce fine wines and the finest olive oils. He's got big plans."

"Good luck to him, then," her father said, sounding hollowed out. Vivian Marsdon knew Costello would achieve everything he had ever wanted. And didn't that include Charlotte, his daughter? "Oh, God, I feel wretched," he mumbled. "I started my married life with such high hopes. I wanted to be loved and admired like my father. I wanted to be a great success. I thought I had inherited his business brain. I didn't, sad to say. I've had to come face to face with the cold, hard facts. I never listened. I made terrible mistakes. It cost us all. And I had to live with your mother's chronic obsession with Mattie and his health."

"Don't upset yourself, Dad. We won't talk about Mattie any more. It's too painful."

"Indeed it is. But we have our Chrissie—the best boy in the world. He's amazingly bright."

Like father. Like son.

"I know *you* were always a top student, Charlie," her father continued, "but Martyn definitely wasn't. He couldn't even get a place at university. He was spoiled rotten—born lazy. Unlike Gordon. Christopher has an exceptionally high IQ. I was thrilled when he was classed as a gifted child."

"And you've brought him on wonderfully, Dad," she said gently. "I'm so grateful you take such an interest in him."

Her father's thick eyebrows shot up. "Good God, girl, he's my grandson."

"Please remember that, Dad," she said very quietly. "Mum has little or no time for him."

Vivian Marsdon moaned in distress. "Her loss, my dear. Chrissie used to look like Matthew, but he doesn't any more. Still, he's a Marsdon. My eyes have faded somewhat, but they used to be very blue. Did you ask Costello how he's made his money? He owns the place outright, doesn't he?"

Charlotte nodded. "He *is* Vortex. I wasn't about to question him, Dad. I don't have the right."

"Blasted revenge—that's what it is." Vivian Marsdon was back to railing. "He's lived to get square. I tell you, I was shocked out of my mind to see him."

"And *I* wasn't?"

"The arrogance of him!" Marsdon fumed. "Always had it—even as a boy."

Charlotte expelled a long breath. "Not arrogance, Dad. Rohan was never arrogant. Rohan *is* what he is. Someone truly exceptional. By temperament a born leader."

Vivian Marsdon drew a deep sigh. Who could deny it? Many a time he had wished for a son like Rohan Costello, at the same time feeling guilty at the very thought. It was as if he were brushing his own son Matthew, a beautiful, sunny-natured boy, aside.

"Well, Costello—unlike me—obviously knows how to make money," he said finally. "But doesn't that prove how little he actually cares about you? You were supposed to be such great friends. Inseparable at one time. He surely could have notified you? Let you know beforehand. Not shocked us both. If that isn't revenge, what is?"

She had absolutely no comeback to that.

CHAPTER FOUR

MONDAY morning. School. The same primary school they had all attended as children. She followed her normal routine, picking up Peter Stafford and his scratchy little sister Angela along the way. Angela was such an unpleasant child sometimes it was hard to believe the two were related.

As always, Charlotte arrived in comfortable time, allowing the boys to settle before classes began. There was welcome shade beneath a flowering gum twenty yards from the front gate. She moved her Mercedes smoothly into the parking spot left by a departing Volvo. The driver, her friend Penny, wiggled a hand out of the window. Penny's little one, Emma, was only in pre-school. Charlotte had been the first to marry and fall pregnant. Or rather the other way about. She wouldn't be the first or the last. But it certainly made her the youngest mother of a Grade 3 child.

"Thank you, Mrs Prescott." Dear little Peter never forgot to thank her, while his sister dashed away without a backward glance.

She watched the boys shoulder their backpacks. "It's always a pleasure, Peter." She smiled affectionately at him. "Now, you two have a good day and I'll see you this afternoon." She touched a farewelling hand to Peter's shoulder, dropped a kiss on her son's head.

"See you, Mummy," Christopher said, his face lighting up with his wonderfully sweet smile.

It tore at her heart. Rohan had smiled at her like that. Once. Christopher's hair was a gleaming blond, like hers, but he didn't have her creamy skin. He had Rohan's olive skin. In summer it turned a trouble-free gold.

She stood watching a minute more as they ran through the open double gates, meeting up with a group of their friends. All weekend Christopher had been as happy and excited as any young boy could be at having met Rohan, who now owned Riverbend. Things might have been a little different had he taken a dislike to the new owner. As it was, he appeared thrilled. It had been Rohan said this; Rohan said that.

She had thought her father might fly off the handle, but oddly enough he'd listened to his grandson with an attentive smile. He would be thinking Christopher was missing his father. That was Martyn. So far her father suspected nothing. She knew her father would always love Christopher, no matter what. But the inevitability of Christopher's real paternity coming out scared her to death. There had never been a scandal attached to the Marsdon name. Martyn had blotted the Prescotts' copybook. She wasn't thinking of herself. She was thinking, as always, of her son. And her father. God knew what her absent mother would make of it! She shuddered to think.

She was about to return to her car when she became aware that a tall, lean, stunning young man, wearing jeans and a navy T-shirt with a white logo, was heading straight for her. Only now could she see the estate's Range Rover a little distance down on the opposite side of the road. He must have been waiting for her.

She stood stock still, willing her heart to stop racing. Her body, which had been calm enough, was now assailed by tingles. She watched him swiftly cross the road. Rohan had always been graceful, beautifully co-ordinated. He hadn't just excelled in the classroom, he had been the Valley's top athlete. Many of the boys had been gifted young sports-men—Martyn had been a fine swimmer, tennis and cricket player. He had wanted to study sports when he finished high school, but he hadn't had the marks. Poor Martyn. His father had put him to work. Well, in a manner of speaking. Martyn had wanted for nothing.

Except *her*. Unrequited love did terrible things to a man.

"Good morning, Rohan." She knew she sounded very formal, but she was concentrating hard on marshalling her strength. "You wanted to see me?"

"I thought we could have a cup of coffee." He was study-ing her as intently as she was studying him.

"I really don't have the time."

"I think you do. A cup of coffee and a friendly chat. Won't keep you long. I've checked out the village. Stefano's?"

She nodded. "It's the best."

"So I'll meet you there?"

Her nerves were drawn so tight they were thrumming like live wires. "I can't imagine not doing what you want, Rohan." She turned away before he could form a retort.

At that time in the morning it was easy to find a parking spot in the main road, outside the popular coffee shop with its attractive awning in broad white and terracotta stripes. Stefano's was owned and run by an Italian family who really knew their business. Coffee was accompanied by selections of little cakes, mini-cheesecakes and pastries. Stefano's also served delicious light lunches. Charlotte and the friends who had remained loyal to her had been frequent customers since the café had opened almost a year before.

This morning she was greeted with a beaming, "*Buon giorno*, Carlotta—Signor Costello." Stefano was a large man, almost bear-like in appearance, but very light on his feet.

"*Buon giorno*, Stefano."

It only then occurred to Charlotte that the de Campo family would have been invited to the Open Day. Obviously Stefano, the grandfather and head of the family, had met Rohan that day. Hence the big flashing smile and the use of his name.

Stefano took their orders after a few pleasantries: long black for Rohan, cappuccino for her, and a small slice each of Signora de Campo's freshly baked Siena cake—a great favourite with the customers.

Charlotte looked across the table, set with a crisp white cloth and a tiny glass vase containing a single fresh flower—a sunshine-yellow gerbera, with an open smiling face. "So, how can I help you, Rohan?"

He just looked at her. He wanted to keep looking at her. Never stop. Her beautiful blonde hair was drawn back from her face, a section caught high with a gold clasp, the rest of her shining mane hanging down her back. She was dressed much as he was, but in a feminine version: jeans—white, in her case—with a pink and white checked shirt, white trainers on her feet. She was wearing no make-up apart from a soft pink lipgloss, so far as he could see. She always had had flawless skin.

"How's Christopher?"

So many emotions were cascading through her. "Full of his new best friend. It's been Rohan this, Rohan that, all weekend," she told him.

"How did your father take that?" His gaze sharpened.

"To be honest—"

"For a *change*," he cut in.

She gave a small grimace and looked away from him into the sunlit street. Two of the school mothers were going into the bookshop opposite. Other villagers were strolling past the coffee shop, one commenting on the luxuriant potted golden canes that flanked the front door.

"Dad loves Christopher," she said, turning her head slowly back to him. "I told you that. He listened and smiled."

"Good grief!" Rohan leaned back in his comfortable chair, eyes sparkling with malice. "Maybe there are miracles after all!"

"One likes to think so. Here comes Stefano."

"Gosh, why the warning?" he asked sardonically. "I thought we looked perfectly relaxed—not raring for a fight."

"*You* might feel relaxed. I don't."

"Charlotte, you look perfectly beautiful and quite normal. A good actress, I guess."

Stefano set the tray down on an adjacent empty table, then unloaded their coffee, placing it before them. The panforte followed, heavily dusted with white icing sugar and showing roasted nuts and a succulent mix of candied peel.

"*Grazie*, Stefano." Rohan nodded in acknowledgement. "This looks good."

"*Altro?*"

"*Nient'altro, grazie.*" Charlotte answered this time, giving the courtly proprietor a warm smile.

It was the first genuine smile Rohan had seen from her in a very, very long time. It wasn't directed at him. He saw Stefano flush with pleasure. Charlotte had never been fully aware of her own beauty and its power.

The coffee was excellent. Stefano glanced back and Rohan gave him the seal of approval with a thumbs-up. Stefano was a great *barista*, and it wasn't all that easy. He savoured another long sip, then leaned back. "I'm having a few guests this coming Saturday. Probably they'll all be here by late afternoon, and will stay over until Sunday. Ten of us in all. Counting you, of course."

She hoped her composed expression didn't change. "Who needs *my* acceptance?" She turned out her palms.

"Come on," he jeered softly. "In the old days you were someone very special in my life. You're about to be reinstated."

She saw the glint in his eyes. "I'm absolutely rapt about that, Rohan. This is blackmail, you know."

His voice hardened. "You'd do well to remember the reason. Try the cake. It looks delicious."

"So what am I supposed to *do*?" she asked after a moment.

"Nothing too onerous. I've given my housekeeper the night off. Ms Rodgers will be looking after the catering. All you have to do is look beautiful and come to dinner Saturday night."

"That's all?" Part of her wanted to tell him she didn't much like his PR woman. She hoped Ms Rodgers wasn't going to play hostess at Riverbend. She didn't think she could take seeing Diane Rodgers sitting where her mother had always sat.

"That's all—apart from an impromptu little after-dinner concert." He raised a black brow at her.

"I'm sorry, Rohan. I'm out of practice." She wasn't. She loved her piano. She was a very good pianist—just like her mother. She had started teaching Christopher the very day he'd shown interest. He'd been five. "Besides, there's the little matter of a piano."

"Solved," he said. "I've had a new Steinway installed. "Even out of practice—which I doubt—an hour or two on that would set you right.'

She had a flashback to the Open Day, when she had fainted. Used to seeing a concert grand in the Drawing Room, in her bemused state she had thought it hers.

"Just a couple of party pieces?" he suggested. "I want to show you off. I intend everyone to know we're back to being *very good friends*!"

Very good friends? "Aren't you rather rushing it?" There was a defiant look in her eyes.

"Not at all." He shrugged. "My friends know I grew up in Silver Valley. They will learn it was your father who sold me Riverbend."

"They don't know now?"

"Only Diane."

"Of course—Diane. Sounds like she runs your life. Am I to take it she'll be a guest at dinner?"

"You know the rules, Charlotte. Even numbers." His tone was sardonic.

"So you have someone for me?"

"I have someone for Diane," he corrected. "*You're* my certain someone, Charlotte. God knows, I've waited all these years, never considering for a moment what you'd been up to."

"Formal or informal dress?" Stoically she ignored his taunting.

"Why, formal—what else? Your parents' dinner parties were always formal. My mother—you know, the hired help—used to tell me how everyone dressed up. How beautiful your mother always looked, the splendid jewellery she wore. In those days my mother thought the world of Mrs Marsdon, the Lady of the Manor."

It gave Charlotte an opening, if nothing else. "How *is* your mother? I wanted so much to ask."

"So why didn't you?'

"I knew right off to exercise extreme caution around you. You've changed, Rohan."

"Alas, I have!" he drawled. "Let me see. Who could have changed me? Changed my life?"

"Fate is as close as I can get." She picked up her coffee before it went cold.

He gave her an insouciant smile. "I have to return to Sydney this afternoon. Back Friday night. I have business meetings lined up."

She gave him an enquiring look. "Dare I ask what line of business you are in?"

"Why not?" He leaned forward. "You remember I was a computer whiz kid?"

"Absolutely. You were a whiz kid at everything," she admitted wryly.

"You might also remember I was searching desperately for a way to make money so I could offer marriage to the girl I *then* loved." The steely glint was back in his eyes. "I was always into computer science, I had a special flair for it. Then it struck me that the quickest way to make money was to try to break into entertainment software. I'd done well enough with educational software, but decided to take the risk of moving to games. Sometimes they don't take off. Mine did. I've never looked back. In no time at all the money started to flow in. I have three companies now that handle multiple software programs. I hire the right people. My employees are all young and brilliant at what they do. I've built businesses around what I and my staff enjoy. They also have the opportunity to buy shares in our companies—share in the profits. They all want to get rich too."

"So you've made millions?" she asked, not at all surprised. He had energy and enterprise written all over him.

"The *reason* I wanted to make millions," he told her tersely, "was to keep *you* in the style you were accustomed to. And, of course, to make life much better and easier for my mother. Which, needless to say, I have."

"And I'm glad, Rohan. Truly glad. Your mother deserves her slice of good fortune. But why ever did you want Riverbend?"

He gave an elegant shrug of his shoulder. Whoever his father was, he must have been a fascinating man. "Simple. I'm always on the lookout for something else. I got started on real estate investing. Real estate, as you know, is one of the best ways to create wealth. Better yet hold on to it for the family I intend to have. Christopher is our *first* child. Hopefully I'll get to hold our second-born child in my arms. It was a dream of mine to have our child."

"It was *our* dream, Rohan." There was no mistaking the injured look in her lustrous green eyes.

"Odd way you went about it."

They were so utterly engrossed in each other they failed to notice the small, dumpy young woman who strode with single-minded purpose to their table.

"Well, well, well!" Nicole Prescott said, her tone coated with layer upon layer of meaning they were obviously meant to guess at.

Charlotte realised at once that Nicole's seeing them together had greatly upset her. Every muscle in her own stomach clenched, as though steeling for the blows that might come. Rohan stood up, looking perfectly self-assured, and at six-three towering over the diminutive Nicole. Nicole could easily have looked so much better, but Charlotte had learned to her cost that Nicole much preferred her image of messy, prolonged adolescence.

"Mind your own business, Charlotte. We can't all look like you!" How many times had she heard that?

"Well, well, well, to you too, Nicole," Rohan said suavely. "Tell me—were you after coffee, or did you see us through the window?" He gave her a brilliant look that fell short of contempt. He had never liked Nicole Prescott. Had little reason to.

A tremor shook Charlotte's whole body. Nicole had always been such an abrasive person, with an oversized chip on her shoulder. It had made her very hurtful. Over the years Nicole had developed such a badly done by expression it had set like cement. Did she intend to make a scene? Nicole was given to hurling insults. She was even cruel. She had done her best to blacken Rohan's name—though, knowing her brother, she must have had serious doubts about Martyn's version of events that fatal afternoon. It all went back to Mattie.

"You just never could keep away from each other," Nicole hissed, literally seething with resentment.

Rohan pitched his voice low, but it carried natural authority and the capacity to act on it. "I would advise you not to make an enemy of me, Nicole."

"That's right—you're *rich* now," she sneered.

"And I have big interests in this valley."

Nicole blinked. *Big interests?* Hadn't her father hinted at some such thing? Not just Riverbend, then? She forced herself to look away from Rohan Costello's burning blue gaze. It transfixed her. Bluer than blue. She heard her mother's voice in her head, *"We don't know. We don't know."* Always handsome, Rohan Costello had matured into the sort of man women couldn't take their eyes off. She had to concentrate now on Charlotte—the weak link.

She had hated beautiful Charlotte Marsdon all her life.
So unfairly blessed. Beauty, charm, brains. She had the lot.
Everyone loved her. Well, *she* hated Charlotte. Had hated
her even when she'd followed Charlotte down the aisle to
join her besotted brother in unholy matrimony—she the
shortest and the plainest of the bridesmaids. Beauty gave a
woman such power. Martyn was the one who had inherited
all the looks. As a kid he had nicknamed her Mousy. It still
stuck in some quarters. But she had triumphed over her
nondescript looks by developing a tongue sharp enough
to cut.

They hadn't been invited to the garden party. She and
her mother had fumed over that. They were the Prescotts.
Not a family to be ignored. Small wonder they were furi-
ous. Her father had simply made the comment, "What did
the two of you expect?"

It was like that these days. Two against one. She and her
mother against her father. He was so unbelievably *tolerant*.
And he had never had much faith or pride in her adored
brother. She would never forgive him for that.

"You knew about all this, didn't you?" She rounded
on Charlotte with the barbed accusation. "You knew he'd
bought Riverbend. You knew he'd had us barred from the
garden party."

"Wrong on both counts, Nicole," Charlotte said. It was
news to her. There was no guarantee Nicole wouldn't start
spewing venom any moment now. Out of the corner of
her eye she could see Stefano, looking their way rather
anxiously.

"I *know* you," Nicole spat. "I know the two of you. Your
history. I know how you broke my brother's heart."

"And we know *you*, Nicole," Rohan responded in a warning voice. "You and Martyn. *Unfortunately*. If you want
a cup of coffee I suggest you consider going elsewhere."

There was a daunting edge to his voice. "We've only just settled in, and Stefano is looking this way with concern."

"Forget him!" Nicole snapped out, but the hard challenge was causing her to crumple like soggy tissue paper. "How's my nephew, by the way?" She shot Charlotte a look of utter loathing.

Charlotte thought her heart might go into spasm. Christopher had to be protected at all costs. She looked beyond Nicole with her puffy cheeks to Rohan, who had made the slightest move forward. "Why don't *we* go?" she suggested quickly. "Nicole is beyond hope."

"*I'm* beyond hope?" Nicole's face took on high colour. She was the one to do the taunting, launch the insults. Not lovely, ladylike Charlotte.

"Probably you know it," Rohan suggested suavely. "I'd go now, Nicole, if I were you. Remember you're a *Prescott*!"

That stopped Nicole more effectively than a jug of cold water. She backed off abruptly, saying scornfully as she went, "Your poor mother—the *cleaning lady*—never did teach you any manners, did she?"

Rohan laughed, as though genuinely amused by the comment. "I've never heard my mother swear—yet *your* mother drops the F-word in every other sentence. I bet you do too."

For once Nicole had no reply. She spun about, and then took off like a bat out of hell.

Rohan sat down again with an exaggerated sigh. "What a gentle little soul she is! A helicopter could spot that chip on her shoulder. All in all, the Prescotts were blessed with their children, wouldn't you say? Nicole's jealousy of you is downright pathological.'

"That's what makes her dangerous, Rohan."

He looked across at her, seeing her distress. "It's okay. Stop worrying. What can she actually do?"

"She's already seized on Christopher's resemblance to you," she said in a deeply concerned voice.

"Christopher's relationship to me *must* come out." His tone hardened.

"But you promised!"

"And I meant it." Frowning, he looked truly formidable. "Nicole and her dreadful mother—how in God's name did you ever live with them?—can suspect all they like. They don't *know*."

"They could offer to take him for a weekend. This is the age of DNA testing." Fear was lodged like a heavy stone against her heart.

"Isn't that good?" he countered with the utmost sarcasm. "Tell them *no*. You've already said they've seen little of you since Martyn's death."

"I like Gordon—Martyn's father. He's the nice one of the family."

"Wasn't Martyn nice enough to marry?"

"Martyn's dead." She veiled her eyes.

"Well, his death is one less cross for you to bear," he pointed out rather callously. "I'm sorry Martyn had to die so young, Charlotte. Once we were friends, until he turned on me with a vengeance. Anything to protect himself. He really was gutless. We both know he had a foolhardy streak that was always going to get him and sadly other people into trouble. You could have divorced him."

"Then I really would have been in trouble." She reacted with an involuntary shudder.

He sat forward, staring at her in consternation. "What is *that* supposed to mean?" His eyes blazed.

She didn't answer. She had said too much already. Did

anyone get through life unscathed? Women particularly? Vulnerable women with children to protect?

"Were you afraid of Martyn? What he might do?"

She shook her head.

"If you ever try to leave me, I'll kill you and the boy."

Martyn's final words to her had played over and over in her head. By now they were driven deep into her psyche. "I must go, Rohan," she pleaded. "There are things I have to do at home."

"You're going to have to talk to me some time." He rose to his splendid height, extracting a couple of notes from his wallet.

She stood up more slowly. "There are some things you don't need to hear, Rohan."

His steely determination—the determination that had turned him at under thirty into a multimillionaire—was well in evidence. "That, Charlotte, is an answer I don't accept."

Life for Charlotte had become an endless series of hurdles.

CHAPTER FIVE

SOMEONE on Rohan's staff was to pick her up at ten to seven. Drinks in the library. Dinner in the formal dining room. Diane Rodgers was handling the catering. Diane Rodgers would be sitting down to dinner. Swanning around Charlotte's former home.

"Why are you doing this?" her father asked, for the umpteenth time.

It wasn't as though she had a choice. "Rohan insisted."

"And you jumped?"

"Only some of the time." She had no protection from Rohan.

"You look *beautiful*, Mummy." Christopher caught his mother's fingers. He didn't like it when Grandpa had words with his mother. "I love it when you let your hair down." He looked up admiringly at his mother's thick golden hair. He was used to seeing her hair tied back, but tonight it fell in lovely big waves around her face and over her shoulders. "I love the dress too," he enthused. "I've never seen it before." It was a long dress of some shiny material. It deepened the colour of his mother's green eyes and made her lovely skin glow.

"You love *everything* about your mother," Vivian Marsdon said with an indulgent smile. He too loved seeing his daughter looking her best. As a boy, like Christopher, he had taken great pleasure in seeing his own mother dress up for an occasion. "You *do* look beautiful, Charlotte." He paused for a moment, considering. "Why don't you wear your grandmother's emeralds?"

"Goodness me, Dad, I don't want to overdo it!" she exclaimed. Her mother had taken the beautiful jewellery her husband had given her, but Grandma Marsdon's jewellery was off-limits. It was to remain in the family.

"Well, I *want* you to," Vivian Marsdon decided. "Damned strangers swanning around in our house." Eerily, he echoed her thoughts.

"You swore, Grandpa," Christopher turned to look at his grandfather. "You know the rules. Swearing isn't allowed." He figured it was time to get one back at Grandpa.

"I'm sorry, son," Vivian apologised. "I'm a bit upset. I'll take the emeralds from the safe, Charlotte. I'd like you to wear them. Keep the flag flying, if you like. I'm sure the other women will be wearing their best jewellery."

"Probably, Dad," she conceded. "But it might be a mite hard to top Gran's emeralds."

"Well, you have the beauty and the style," he said, already moving off to his study, where the safe was installed. "Besides, they'll go perfectly with that dress. Green is your colour."

Rohan, looking devastatingly handsome in black tie, greeted her at the door. "Ah, Charlotte! You look a vision of beauty!"

She brought herself quickly under control. It wasn't easy when she was on an emotional see-saw. Fear. Elation. She couldn't get over having Rohan back in her life. It was like some impossible dream. Her love for him had never lost its intensity, even through the unhappy years of her marriage. She had given up the love of her life for Martyn, whose actions had determined the course of all three of their lives. She rarely let her mind travel back to Martyn's unwitting part in Mattie's tragedy. She had never, ever upbraided Martyn for it. Only for his part in denouncing Rohan to anyone who would listen. Martyn hadn't been a strong character. He had known that and suffered for it.

Now Rohan's brilliant eyes glittered over her and touched on the emeralds, no more dazzling than her eyes. He bent his dark head to brush her cheek. Her heart turned over. The clean male scent of him! He took the opportunity to murmur in her ear. "Ah, the famous Marsdon emeralds. They look glorious! But no more than you!"

"Why, thank you, Rohan." She had become fairly adept at pretending cool composure. "That's what Dad was hoping for. 'Fly the flag' were his exact words."

"And how triumphantly it's unfurled! Come on in." He took her hand, his long fingers curling around hers. Electricity shot up her arm, branched away into her throat, her breast, travelled to the sensitive delta of her body. She felt the impact of skin on skin at every level. "Meet my guests," he was saying smoothly. "I'm sure you'll like them, and they you. Still think losing Riverbend is tragic?" His downbent head pinned her gaze.

"Not any more. I only wanted it for Christopher anyway."

"Then your prayers have been answered," he returned sardonically.

Diane Rodgers had marked their entry. Immediately she was seized by a jealousy so powerful it was a wonder she didn't moan aloud. She felt so completely engulfed by it, it was like drowning in mortal sin. If there was such a thing. They looked *perfect* together. Stunning foils for each other. Charlotte Prescott looked *beyond* glamorous—and looking glamorous was her own crowning achievement. Up until now she had thought she looked terrific in her short mesh and sequin dress. Hell, she *did* look terrific. But Mrs Prescott looked *fabulous*—a walking, breathing, real-live beautiful woman. The long dress, clinging and dipping in all the right places, put her in mind of the emerald silk number Keira Knightley had worn in the movie *Atonement*. If that weren't enough, a magnificent diamond and emerald necklace was strung around her neck like a glittering tie, caught by a big dazzling emerald clasp of God knew how many carats. The full length of the separate strands dipped into her creamy cleavage.

Hell!

Diane looked furtively about her. She had an idea she might have exclaimed aloud.

She couldn't have. No one responded. Not that they were looking in her direction. They were staring at the beauty on Rohan's arm. One thing offered a grain of consolation. Mrs Prescott's late husband—a bit of a playboy, she'd heard—had been having an affair at the time of his fatal accident. A young woman had been with him in his luxury Maserati. The miracle was she hadn't joined her boyfriend. So the beauteous Mrs Prescott hadn't been able to hang on to her husband! She had lost him. Diane half believed that gave her hope.

The only other times she had seen Charlotte Marsdon, her long hair had been confined. Now it billowed away from her face, revealing matching diamond and emerald earrings. Who the hell could compete with that? It was utterly demoralising. Her mood turned from super-confident to darkly brooding.

"Geez, isn't she *fan-taas-tic*!" Sam Bailey turned his smooth brown head to give her a cat-like grin.

Diane Rodgers was tempted to crack him on the nose;

instead she met his look head-on. "Gorgeous!" she agreed, feeling as if she was under siege.

She had never much liked Sam Bailey. Now she hated him and his playful little taunts. At least she *thought* they were playful. She'd been certain she'd been keeping her wild infatuation with the dead sexy Rohan under wraps. Apparently not. Rohan Costello had got right under her skin at first sight, and she prided herself on her street cool. Were they all laughing at her? God, that would be catastrophic! She couldn't ask Sam—he was making a bee-line for his boss and the exquisite Mrs Prescott. What a hell of a pity the husband was dead. But playboys given to driving fast cars sadly tended to die young.

Diane had done an impressive job of handling the arrangements. Charlotte awarded her top marks. If she hadn't exactly done things herself, then she had the knack of gathering together the right people. The flower arrangements in the entrance hall and the main reception rooms were stunning. A quartet of sumptuous yellow roses, their lovely full heads massed in crystal bowls, were set at intervals along the dining table. She had never seen the impressive gold and white dinner set before, but she recognised Versace. The dinner plates were flanked by sterling silver flatware. Georgian silver candlesticks marched apace. Trios of exquisite crystal wine glasses were set at the head of the dinner plates.

Food and drink turned out to be superb, as did the efficient and unobtrusive service from two good-looking, nattily uniformed young waiters. Perfectly moulded smoked salmon and prawn timbales topped with a slice of cucumber and a sprig of coriander for starters; a choice of beef fillet with wild mushrooms and a mushroom vinaigrette or chicken with peaches and vanilla; crêpes with walnut cream and butterscotch sauce or chocolate cherry liqueur cake. It was a truly elegant and satisfying feast.

Conversation flowed easily, ranging over a number of interesting and entertaining topics—all non-divisive. Charlotte found it much easier than she had anticipated. She had never been to Riverbend as a guest. Rohan presided at the head of the table, she to his right. The guest of honour. She wondered what they all thought. Curiously, she felt relaxed—even with Diane Rodgers shooting her many a burning look of appraisal that bit hostile.

She had attended countless dinner parties over the years, but she found herself enjoying Rohan's quick-witted and amusing guests more than most. It was obvious they thought the world of him. Their friend as well as their boss. They were all of an age. Three of the young men and two of the very attractive young women, not including Diane Rodgers, worked for Rohan. Two of the young men were computer whiz kids and had brought their girlfriends along.

Rohan's guests knew better than to start asking leading questions. Except for Diane who, over coffee and liqueurs in the Drawing Room, decided it was high time to throw the cat among the pigeons. For starters there was the enthralling subject of their shared childhood. Charlotte's and Rohan's.

"I bet Rohan was an A-grade student," she said, setting down her exquisite little coffee cup so she could lap up the answer.

Charlotte smiled, wondering where this was going. "The cleverest boy in the Valley," she said, without looking at Rohan. "We all knew he was going to make a huge success of himself."

"Whereas you settled for being a wife and mother?" Diane said, her voice full of womanly understanding. "Possibly the best job of all. You must have been very young when you had your gorgeous little boy. He's—what? Seven?"

"Yes, he is. And he *is* beautiful," Charlotte agreed, hoping Diane would stop. Rohan might look perfectly at ease, lounging back in his armchair, but she knew him so well she could sense a growing turbulence.

"You married another one of your childhood friends— Martyn Prescott, I believe?" Diane pressed on where angels would fear to tread. "Isn't that right? What were you called again? The Gang of Four?"

Charlotte's heart plunged. She was certain Diane Rodgers had talked to Nicole Prescott. "The *Pack* of Four, Diane. But I think you already knew that."

Rohan broke in crisply. "I'm sure Charlotte doesn't want to continue the interrogation, Diane. But *I'm* rather interested to know who told you about the Pack of Four."

Diane's colour deepened. "Gosh, I can't remember," she said, with an innocent blink of her heavily made up dark eyes. "I thought it was a lovely story, anyway. I'm sorry if I've upset you, Charlotte. I just wasn't thinking." Her voice dripped apology.

"That's quite all right, Diane." Charlotte maintained her cool calm. Maybe Diane was on the level? Anything was possible. "I lost my husband eighteen months ago," she told the table. They murmured their sympathy, all of them embarrassed by Diane's insensitivity. At least three of the guests could have told Charlotte that Diane Rodgers could be obnoxious.

"Sorry. So sorry." Diane pressed a hand to her mouth, then thought she had nothing to lose. "I know you've had more than your fair share of tragedy."

Down the table, Sam Bailey rolled his eyes. "Is that silly bitch into annihilation? If she doesn't shut her mouth soon she could just find herself out of a well-paid job," he muttered to his girlfriend, who was in total agreement. They all knew Diane Rodgers was highly effective—she was devoted to their boss and very capable—but the dumbest person on the planet could diagnose an attack of monster jealousy when they saw it.

Some time later, Charlotte took her place at the piano—to delighted applause.

"Do you want the lid up?" Rohan asked, aware Diane had upset Charlotte. Which meant she had upset him, too. Anyone would think he'd been sleeping with Diane, so apparent was her jealousy.

"Not right up," Charlotte said. "I don't want to rocket my audience out of the room." Spacious as the Drawing Room was, this was a nine-foot concert grand.

"This just gets better and better!" Sam exclaimed, settling onto one of the sofas beside his girlfriend and taking her hand. He was blown away by the magnificence of Riverbend. For that matter blown away by the beautiful daughter of the former owner. There was quite a story there.

"I'm a little out of practice," Charlotte turned on the long piano seat to confess. "I've chosen the lovely 'Levitski Waltz'. You may not know the name, but I'm sure you will know the melody, and a couple of shortish pieces from Albéniz's *Suite Española*."

"*Olé!*" Irrepressible Sam essayed a burst of flamenco clapping. Rohan's Charlotte was simply sensational. Why not? So was his boss.

Charlotte waited until they were all seated comfortably, Rohan at their centre. Then she turned back to the Steinway. She was certain Rohan would have had it tuned to perfect pitch after it had been shifted into the house.

To be on the safe side she made a short exploration of the beautiful instrument's dynamics.

"What the hell is she doing?" Diane had to ask the question, feeling a stab of dismay. She wasn't into classical music. She fluffed out her shiny bob. "Is that it?" she whispered to the young woman beside her.

"Get real!" was the astonished response. "Charlotte is just warming up."

"Yeah—I was just having a little joke," said Diane, trying to prove she was as clued-up as the rest of them. She knew Rohan loved classical music. She had seen many of his CDs. Piano, violin, opera singers, symphony orchestras. You name it. Difficult when she had a passion for rock. Something *hot*!

When at last the beautiful, talented Mrs Prescott's little recital came to an end Diane muttered to herself, *"Thank you, God!"* She felt sure Charlotte had been showing off. Closed eyes. Bowed head. That business with her raised hands. *Showing off.* The waltz hadn't been too bad. But she'd had no compulsion to tap her toes at the Spanish numbers. Needless to say that smart alec Sam the sycophant had. It had really pained her to mark the expression on Rohan's handsome face. It suggested he had been transported to some celestial plain. Okay, he adored classical music. Probably that was his only fault.

The party broke up around twelve-thirty. Rohan's guests started to make their way upstairs, having told Charlotte how much they'd enjoyed meeting her and congratulating her on her lovely performance at the piano. Rohan's Charlotte was a true musician.

Last in line, Diane bit her lip so hard she very nearly drew blood. "I hope you enjoyed yourself, Charlotte?" she said, with a bright hostess look.

"Very much so." Charlotte smiled. "I must congratulate you on arranging everything so beautifully, Diane."

"All in a day's work!" Diane's expression turned suitably modest. "I'll say goodnight, then. Will we be seeing you tomorrow?" It wasn't as though the Prescott woman didn't have plenty of time to squander, she thought.

"I doubt it," Charlotte replied lightly. "Goodnight, Diane."

"Goodnight." Diane revved up a smile even though she was so angry. "Goodnight, Rohan."

God, he had to be the sexiest man on the planet. Maybe too sexy for his own good? She had an overwhelming urge to grab him and press him to her throbbing bosom. She had convinced herself she was worthy of Rohan Costello, although she knew he came with a warning. This was a guy who broke hearts. Not intentionally, was the word. But he hadn't been serious about any one of the highly attractive young women he had dated in the past. It distressed her terribly to have Charlotte Prescott, the widow, re-emerge.

Rohan gave her the smile she adored. Did he have any idea how sexy he was? "Goodnight, Diane. Everything went very well."

"Why, thank you!" Diane saw herself as the very image of indefatigable efficiency. She waggled her fingers, then started to move off towards the grand staircase, carrying the heavy weight of jealousy. She paused and turned back for a moment, focusing her gaze on Charlotte. "Look, why don't we catch up some time, Charlotte?" she suggested, making it sound as though they had hit it off wonderfully well. Kindred spirits, as it were.

"You want to keep her under observation?" Rohan asked suavely.

Diane wasn't sure if that was a joke or not. Rohan was such a man of mystery.

Charlotte was kinder. "I'll keep it in mind, Diane."

"Lovely!" Diane threw in another brilliant hostessy smile.

They remained silent until they saw Diane moving gracefully up the staircase on her very high heels.

Charlotte felt rather sorry for Diane. She didn't blame her for falling for Rohan. He was magnetic enough to draw any woman. She had caught Sam Bailey in particular having little snickers at Diane's expense. Diane wasn't liked, it seemed. But she *was* efficient. And very vulnerable where her boss was concerned.

"Now, there's a woman who would like to own you," she said wryly.

"Good thing she hasn't told *me*," was Rohan's brisk reply. "Will we walk back to the Lodge, or won't your evening sandals take it?" He glanced down at her beautifully shod narrow feet. "We can go through the garden. Or I can drive you."

"The drive might be safer."

"Oh, don't be ridiculous!" His tone was derisive. "Nobody said anything about sex," he taunted.

"But you're planning on having it soon?" She rounded on him, lustrous green eyes sparking a challenge.

"Well, we always were compatible in that area," he said, taking her arm. "So—a walk, or the Range Rover?'

"The garden," she said. "It's quickest and the easiest."

His brilliant gaze moved searchingly over her, as though he could uncover her every thought, her every secret. "I can't promise I'll make a point of sticking to the paths."

She put a hand to her throat, as though her heart had suddenly leapt there. Punishment she deserved. The day of reckoning wasn't far off. And then there was Rohan's mother, Mary Rose, deprived of her only grandchild.

Mea culpa!

* * *

A lovely soothing breeze lapped at her hair and her skin, at the fluid long skirt of her evening gown. It wrapped her body and caressed her ankles. The familiar scents of a thousand roses and creamy honeysuckle hung in the air. Above them the stars glittered and danced in a sky of midnight blue velvet. This wasn't wise. But then she had never been able to command wisdom. An aching throb was building up fast in her body.

"Shouldn't you have brought a torch?" she asked, afraid she was revealing too much of her inner agitation.

"For *you*? For *me*?" He gave an edgy laugh. "We know every inch of this place. Don't twist away from me."

"Ah, Rohan!" She gave vent to a deep tremulous sigh that managed to be incredibly seductive. For all their time apart, she was still in thrall to him. Once married to Martyn, she had tried very hard to exorcise Rohan's powerful image. Only it had haunted her every day of her life. And then, as her adored little son had grown older, Rohan's features and mannerisms had begun to emerge! The *fear* she had felt when that occurred! The outright panic. God help her—she had married the *wrong* man! Martyn wasn't the father of her child.

How horrendously rash she had been. She hadn't allowed herself enough time. Only back then she hadn't known what else to do. So young. Pregnant. And she couldn't think Martyn, her friend from childhood, wicked for having physically overcome her. She'd known before they had started out to a rock concert that evening how badly Martyn wanted her. For years he had wanted to be more than just her friend. Only there had always been Rohan. Rohan—who couldn't offer the financial security and the lifestyle he could.

So Martyn had watched and waited for *his* moment.

When she'd realised she was pregnant how she had longed for a wise, loving mother to turn to—a mother full of unconditional love, full of advice as to which course she should take. Her father hadn't been ready for any more shocks. Her escape routes had all been cut off. There had seemed no other course than to pay for her mistake.

Rohan's hand on her tightened, startling her out of her melancholy. "You know it's cruel in its way," he began conversationally. "One can kill trust, respect, write off the crime of betrayal, but one can never kill sexual attraction. I want you very badly—which you damn well know. But then, ours was a very passionate relationship, wasn't it, Charlotte? While it lasted, that is."

Even as he spoke, he could feel the hot blood coursing through his veins. How could he punish Charlotte? Countless times he had longed to be in a position to do so. He had even bought Riverbend, putting in an outrageous offer almost as soon as it came on the market. Revenge on the Marsdons? Revenge on Charlotte who had betrayed him with Martyn, of all people? The only massive impediment was that he wanted her no matter what she did. Charlotte had taken possession of the deepest part of his being.

They walked through a tunnel hung with lovely wisteria towards the summer house, designed as a small Grecian-style temple portico. It glowed whitely ahead. The four classical columns that supported the stone structure were garlanded with a beautiful old-fashioned rose that put out great romantic clusters of cream and palest yellow fragrant blooms, with dark green glossy leaves. Her mother had used to call it the Bourbon rose.

She had a feeling of being inwardly lit up with desire—languorous on the one hand, on the other highly alert. The radiance she felt was so intense it surely must be showing in the luminescence of her skin. She stumbled just a little in her high-heeled sandals. He gripped her arm.

"Oh, Lord!" came from Rohan under his breath. "You were the *world* to me." He hauled her very tightly into his arms. "I lived for you. For our future together."

She was desperate to make amends. "Rohan, I thought—"

He cut her off. "I *don't* want to hear. Remember how we used to come to this place? In secret? This was our shrine, remember? The place of our spiritual and sexual exploration."

"Rohan, I loved you with all my heart."

"Yet you betrayed me."

"I told you. I deserved punishment." She was trembling so badly she needed his tall, lean body to balance her. So much she'd had to endure over the past years. She wanted to cry her heart out. Swear that what she would confess would be the truth, the whole truth, and nothing but the truth.

His grip was fierce and unrelenting. "Well, I have you *now*," he breathed, taking a silky massed handful of her hair and tilting her face up to him. "Come on, Charlotte. Kiss me like you used to."

It was a taunt, a torment. Never an invitation. As in everything he took the initiative. "You're never going to go away, Charlotte."

"No." She was breathless.

"Say it."

"I'm never going to go away. I'll never leave you."

"As if I haven't heard that before." His voice was unbearably cynical. "Only this time we have our son."

Oh, Rohan, hold me. Hold me.

It was an old, old prayer for when she was in a hopeless, helpless situation.

He let go of her long hair, his hands moving to cup her face, his fingers pressing into the fine bones of her skull.

His kiss fell intently on her mouth. Only she confounded him by opening it fully, like a flower to the rain, admitting his seeking tongue to the moist interior. There was no end to sensation, the rush of desire, the rediscovery of rapture. No end to the richness, the incredible *lushness* of sensual pleasure. She reached up naked arms to lock them around his neck. Their darting tongues met in an age-old love dance. She could feel his hands on her, trembling. This had to be a dream from which she never wanted to wake. The first time since the last time she had come blazingly alive. More extraordinarily, the bitterness she knew she had caused, the torture of years of thinking himself betrayed, were nowhere. Not in his mouth. Not in his hands. Profound passion came for them at an annihilating rush.

His hand sought and found her breast, forefinger and thumb stimulating the already tightly budded nipple.

She moaned in mindless rapture, throwing back her head as he kissed her throat.

Oh, the depths of passion! Not even suffering could blunt them.

She could feel herself dissolving. He her captor; she his. She yearned for him…yearned for him… This was her once-in-a-lifetime great love. Desire beat like a drum. It gained power. Surrender would come swiftly behind it. Soon all sense of place would vanish with their clothes. Passion demanded flesh on flesh.

Somehow she found the strength to put a restraining hand over the caressing hand that was palming the globe of her breast. Another second of this and she would be lost to the world.

He must have felt the same way, because he stopped the arousing movement of his hand, letting his hot cheek fall against hers, encountering the wetness of her tears. He savoured them, licking them off with his tongue. They had both been moving with tremendous momentum towards the point of no return.

"All right," he acknowledged, trying to subsume his own near-ungovernable arousal. "I want you for the *night*. Not just minutes out of time."

"Rohan, I can't—"

He cut her off. "You'll have to come to *me*," he said, his voice picking up strength and determination. "Not here. Not Riverbend. I realise the difficulties. But Sydney. Next weekend I've been invited to a big charity function. You'll come as my partner. I'll leave it to you to explain it to your father and Christopher."

She tried to focus on rearranging the bodice of her beautiful silk gown. The flesh of her breast still tingled from his touch. At the very portal of surrender she had pulled back, though she knew her sex-starved body would have no peaceful rest that night.

"It would upset Dad quite a bit," she managed after a while.

"Do you think that bothers me?" His answer was full of disdain. "Your fine, upstanding parents gave my mother and me hell. The only person I'm concerned about is Christopher. I'm only guessing, but I think he'll take it rather well. You're a beautiful young woman, Charlotte. You can't go the rest of your life alone. Or were you planning on living with Daddy for ever?"

"I don't deserve that, Rohan," she shot back. "It's been very difficult. Martyn's death. Dad so sad and lonely. He needed me, Rohan. I couldn't refuse him. I went on to finish my Arts degree externally. I didn't give up. I know I could get myself a halfway decent job in the city, but here in the Valley it would be difficult. No teaching jobs, for instance. All taken. Then there's the fact Chrissie loves the Valley. He loves Dad. I'd hate to uproot him, and I'd have the difficult job of finding a suitable minder for holidays and after-school hours. Not easy!"

"No." He saw the difficulties. "But you don't have to worry now. That's all been taken care of. Our son needs his father."

"I can't let you browbeat me, Rohan." Out of the blue Martyn and his treatment of her popped sickeningly into her mind.

But Rohan was no Martyn.

"*Browbeat* you?" He looked down at her, aghast. "As if I would or could. You want me as much as I want you. That was always the way. Who do you think you're kidding, Charlotte?"

She could feel the tears coming on again. "I've had no *self*, Rohan! Do you understand? No *self*."

He was shaken by the very real agony in her voice. "Did you think you could learn to love Martyn?" He was trying desperately to understand.

"I *loathed* him!" She thrust away. This was dangerous. She had to get home.

"Loathed him?" Rohan was stunned. "What did he do to make you loathe him? Martyn was mad about you. You *loathed* him? Come on, now. I need to know why."

She tossed back her long mane that tumbled in gleaming disarray over her shoulders, struggling hard to come up with an answer that might stave off a confrontation. "You know Martyn wasn't the strongest of characters. His mother pampered him all his life. Rendered him useless. I don't want to talk about Martyn. He's dead, and in some way I am to blame."

He stood stock still, wishing she were under a spotlight so he could look deep into her eyes. "You couldn't possibly have been frightened of Martyn?" He was forced to consider what he had never considered before. Martyn had adored Charlotte. He would never have hurt her. Would he? "I know he could be a bit of a bully, but you could always handle him. Remember how he bullied that little Thomas kid? I threatened to knock the living daylights out of him if he didn't lay off the kid. First and last time I ever threatened anyone. When you married Martyn you put yourself in the Prescotts' power. And Martyn's father was always a decent man."

"The past is past, Rohan," she said, low-voiced. "Neither of us can change it."

"So you *won't* talk?"

"There's nothing to talk about any more," she insisted. "If I could undo the past I would."

Rohan groaned like a man desperate for peace of mind. "I'm not following this at all. If you seriously believed Martyn was Christopher's father— and that's *your* story— you were having sex with both of us."

"I was so *alone*." *Unprotected. Isolated.* "You took that computer job in Western Australia. It couldn't have been further away. I know they offered you a lot of money, but that meant you were gone for the entire summer vacation. I was without you for the best part of four months. I can't talk about this any more, Rohan. I betrayed you. I betrayed myself. I made a terrible mess of my life. But I'm begging for a ceasefire. You've told me what you want. I understand. I want to make it up to you for your suffering."

Rohan raised a staying hand. "Oh, be damned to that, Charlotte!" he said, very sombrely. "Thing is, you *can't*. I understand your wanting the continuation of your privileged lifestyle. Pregnancy would have made you very vulnerable. You were so young. But I can't forgive you for depriving me of my son, depriving my innocent, hard-working mother of her grandson. You do well to cry. Now, I'd better get you home. Daddy will be waiting up for his golden girl."

CHAPTER SIX

JUST as she feared, her father made strenuous objections to her spending the following weekend in Sydney.

"You've always been in Costello's power!" he ranted. "You'd think the boy was some powerful sorcerer. He's always had your heart and your mind."

How true! She and Rohan had connected from early childhood on some profoundly crucial wavelength. "He's not a *boy* any longer, Dad," she pointed out. "He's very much a man. I'm twenty-six, remember? I want a life."

"Not with Costello." Vivian Marsdon violently shook his head. "Never with Costello. The idea is *monstrous*! What would it do to your mother?"

Charlotte's caught her father's eyes. "Do you mean the mother who so cherishes me and my little son?" she asked with considerable pain. "Mum took herself out of our lives. Why should I now worry what *she* thinks?"

"Because you always did and you always will. We both care. I still love Barbara. And you still love your mother, no matter how badly she let us down."

"What about Christopher, Dad?" Charlotte asked heatedly. "*You'll* always love him? No matter what?"

Vivian Marsdon frowningly picked up on her words. "No matter what? What are we talking about, here? Have you formed some new understanding with Costello?"

"There's so much you don't know, Dad. At the heart of it is the sad fact you never *wanted* to know. If Rohan could get me at the snap of a finger, why do you suppose I married Martyn?"

Vivian Marsdon's thick sandy blond eyebrows drew together in a ferocious frown. "Because he loved you. God, Charlie, he was *madly* in love with you. You were all things to him. I scarcely need mention he was in a position to offer you far more than Costello ever could. Security counts with a woman."

"You mean what he could offer *at the time*? It wasn't Martyn's money anyway. The truth is, Dad, Martyn and I lived off his father. They wanted it that way. I wasn't allowed a job outside organising social events. And there was nothing, absolutely nothing, I could do."

Vivian Marsdon stumbled back into his vast armchair. "I don't believe this."

"That's because you've spent your life hiding your head in the sand. It's safer down there."

"It's what I *believed*, Charlie, but I see now I was wrong. I was fearful for your mother's sanity. I couldn't bring myself to take a stand against her. God, I loved her. She was my *wife*. We were happy in the old days. Before our darling Mattie died."

"I know, Dad." Charlotte bowed her head. Nothing good had come out of Mattie's tragic death. But for years of her childhood up until that point it *had* been a magic time. And most of that magic had been due to Rohan Costello.

"But *you* don't have to be alone, Charlie. You're a very beautiful, highly intelligent young woman. You're *my* daughter. A Marsdon. That name still carries a lot of clout. I could name a dozen young men in the Valley desperate to pound their way to your door."

She laughed. "Not a few of them you didn't frighten off, Dad. Good thing I wasn't interested in any of them."

"Why would you be?" he snorted. "Ordinary. Ordinary young men. Costello *isn't*, whatever else he is. He's bought Riverbend on *your* account!" He said it as though he had hit on an invisible truth.

"Rohan bought Riverbend because he's a very astute businessman. It's prime real estate, Dad. The most beautiful estate in a beautiful prosperous valley. Rohan has big plans."

"And they surely include you," Vivian Marsdon said with a sinking heart.

"That upsets you so dreadfully, Dad?"

He looked across at her mournfully. "I couldn't bear to lose you and Chrissie, Charlotte. I have no one else."

"But you won't be losing either of us, Dad," she said, with a burst of love and sympathy. "As long as that's what you want, I would never deprive my boy of his grandfather. He *loves* you."

"He does. God has blessed me. And I love my grandson with all my heart. He's a wonderful little boy. He's going to make his mark in the world. And I didn't think much of Costello's trying to buy the boy's affection by taking him and young Peter for that helicopter ride."

"Oh, come on now, Dad. They were absolutely thrilled. Chris had all the kids madly envious when he told them about it at school. Chris went with Rohan very willingly."

Vivian Marsdon sighed. "I ask you—how did it happen? You'd think Christopher had known him all his life," he added with amazement. "Of course a helicopter ride is a sure way to get to a seven-year-old's heart."

"See it as Christopher learning new things, Dad. He's

only a little boy, but he's a good judge of a person's character. Children see very clearly."

"Especially the latest in helicopters," Marsdon grunted. "It sounds very much to me as though you and Costello have an agenda of your own. How did it happen in such a very short time? I mean, he's only just back in your life. You fainted when you saw him, you were so distressed. Are you really over your husband? What will the Prescotts think if you two get together?"

Charlotte's clear voice hardened. "The only Prescott you have any time for, Dad, is Gordon Prescott. Don't pretend you respected Martyn."

Her father shifted uncomfortably. "I truly believe the only reason he was unfaithful to you, Charlie, was because you didn't love him as he wished."

"Dad, you could be right." Her expression was a mix of self-disgust and sorrow. "I have to tell you I never loved Martyn. It was all a big cover-up. I was pregnant when I married him."

Her father gave vent to another deep sigh. "Yes, well… All the more reason for you to have tried very hard to make a go of it."

"I *did* try, Dad. Not easy pretending you love someone when you don't."

Vivian Marsdon sat with a mournful expression carved into his handsome face. "Your mother didn't beat about the bush with me. She took off."

"It was Riverbend—the river, Dad." She tried to console him.

"Yet we still see Mattie walking by the river, don't we?" He lifted his head to give her the saddest smile. "The river doesn't torture us. In mysterious ways it comforts us. Mattie is close by. Our Chrissie feels Mattie's presence. I never thought much about a *soul* until we lost Mattie. But now

I'm certain we do have one. Never thought much about God. Unlike your mother, I now know there is one. Mattie's *spirit* is here. And it's not a sad one. Wherever he is, Mattie is happy. Remember that strange woman who came to stay outside the village some years back? Always dressed like the old idea of a gypsy? She stopped me once to ask the name of the other child who was with little Christopher and me."

"I remember your account of the incident vividly. The woman claimed she saw a blond boy, on the frail side, aged about fourteen, walking along with you."

"That's right." Vivian Marsdon covered his face with his hand. "It shocked me at the time, but then I realised someone must have told her about Mattie in the village."

"That *could* have happened, Dad, but I don't think it did. She'd only just arrived. Besides, it would have been very cruel to approach you in that way, and you saw no sign of her being anything like that. She kept herself to herself while she was living in that old cottage that had belonged to a relative, and the very last thing people did was bring up our family tragedy. Everyone knew the grief and suffering it had brought down on our heads. Who knows? Maybe she did have a genuine gift. I'm open-minded about such things. You are too. We all *see* Mattie. He's not a trillion miles away. Some part of him is still here, in the place where he lost his mortal life."

"Your mother couldn't bear the thought," Vivian Marsdon said. 'But it comforts me to think that woman might have been saying it the way she saw it."

"Me too." Charlotte reached out for her father's hand.

"You're a good girl, Charlie. *My* girl." He took his handkerchief from his pocket, then strenuously blew his nose. "So, you're going to Sydney for the weekend?"

"I am."

"Have you told Chrissie?"

"Not before I'd spoken to you."

Vivian sank further into his armchair. "I have the feeling he won't have any objection. There could be another helicopter ride in store for him."

Charlotte waited until she had dropped off Peter and his little monster of a sister at their front gate. Peter stood and waved. Angela, as was her custom, ran inside without any acknowledgement of the ride. Then she waited until Peter too was safely inside his front gate. They watched him walking up the short drive.

"Gosh, she's an awful kid!" Christopher made a funny whooping noise. "The rudest kid I know." He was amazed by Angela's behaviour. "Do you suppose she's going to spend her whole life in a bad mood? Peter tells his mother how rude she is, but even Mrs Stafford doesn't seem able to get Angie to say thank you."

"Hopefully it's just a phase." Charlotte patted her son's small hand. The shape of it was Rohan's. "I've something to ask you," she said, keeping her eyes on the road. Safety was all-important. Martyn had been such a careless driver, even when he'd had her and their precious child on board. "Rohan has asked me to be his partner at a big charity function in Sydney this coming Saturday night."

"Really?" Christopher's radiant blue eyes grew huge. "Gee, he's a fast worker," he said, with real admiration.

"If you don't want me to go, I won't." Charlotte meant it.

Christopher laughed. "Don't be silly. I think it's great! I really like Rohan. I want him to be our friend. He's so clever. He'd make a great teacher. He knows tons of things. More than Grandpa, I think. I'd never say that to Gramps, though. Rohan knows all about vineyards and olive groves too. He has lots of plans for Riverbend. He told me I could be in on all of them. Honestly, Mum, I can't think of anyone better than Rohan to go out with. It's sad, the way you're always stuck at home. You looked so beautiful the other night. Rohan thought so too."

"Did he tell you?" She felt the heat in her cheeks.

"Sure he told me. He told me all about when you were kids. You were the greatest friends. He told me really, *really* nice things about you and Uncle Mattie."

She bit her lip. "And about your—father? About Daddy?"

"No, not about Daddy," Christopher admitted. "But Rohan is so easy to talk to I nearly told him I didn't think Daddy liked me."

"What?" Charlotte felt her every nerve in her body stretch to breaking point.

"I *didn't* say anything," Christopher swiftly reassured her, suddenly looking upset. "But Daddy didn't like me much, did he? Not like Grandpa loves me. Nothing like *you* love me. You love me to bits!"

"You can bet on that!" Charlotte spoke with great fervour. "But Daddy did love you, Chrissie," she said, deeply distressed.

"No, Mum." He shook his head. "I don't want you to tell a big fat lie to make me feel better. None of them seemed to care about me. Maybe Grandfather Prescott did. He was always nice. But Grandma Prescott and Nicole—they sure weren't very nice to me. Especially Nicole. I reckon Angela will grow up to be a person just like Nicole. Then there's Grandma Marsdon. She doesn't want to see me. Maybe she thinks you shouldn't have had me in the first place?"

"Christopher, my darling boy! You've been thinking all these things?" She was shocked and appalled. Her son was only seven years old, but already he was weighing up things in his head like an adult.

"Don't worry about it, Mummy." His expression turned protective. "I don't actually care about them any more. Some of the kids tease me about how you and I live with Grandpa. They say things like, 'Why doesn't your mum get married again?' That sort of thing. It annoys me a bit, but it makes Pete *really* angry. He's my friend."

Charlotte's heart gave a great lunge. "You've never told me any of this before. I thought you told me everything?" She felt very sad.

"I didn't tell you because I knew it would upset you. But Rohan's *great*!" Enthusiasm was renewed. "I'm wishing and wishing you two hit it off."

So without even trying Rohan had found a powerful ally.

In his *son*.

Charlotte found as much excitement in the helicopter ride as Christopher would. It was fantastic to see the beautiful rural landscape become a cityscape unfolding beneath them. With the helicopter's wraparound glass the visibility was everything one could wish for, and the Harbour looked magnificent on that special Saturday morning.

It was impossible for her not to feel a surge of pride at the first sight of their beautiful capital city and the iconic "Coathanger"—which was what Sydneysiders called the Sydney Harbour Bridge. The world's largest steel arched bridge, it linked the Sydney CBD and the South and North Shores, with their famous beaches. And down there, jutting out into the sparkling blue waters of Bennelong Point, was one of the great wonders of the modern world: the Sydney Opera House, its famous roof evocative of a ship at full sail.

It couldn't have been more appropriate for the Harbour City, Charlotte thought, though the distinguishing "sails" had cost a great fortune and a whole lot of heartache. But there it was today, in all its splendour. Probably the nation's most recognisable image.

Their pilot Tim Holland, a very experienced and highly respected pilot, was retained by Rohan for personal *and* company use. On Rohan's instructions he took them on a short joyride to increase Charlotte's pleasure. Yachts were out aplenty. The Harbour bloomed with a profusion of white sails. Below them a crowd swam and frolicked in the legendary Bondi surf. Others lay out on the golden sand, sunbaking. Charlotte hoped they were slathered in sunblock. Sydney was Australia's oldest, largest and most culturally diverse city. It was also the most exciting, with an unmatchable *buzz*. She could feel her spirits, for so long down, soaring.

Rohan used his state-of-the-art headset with its voice-activated microphone to speak with her and their pilot, Tim. The headsets enabled them to easily communicate.

"American Airmen during the Second World War flew a couple of Kittyhawks under the Bridge. Not to be outdone, the following year a *flight* of RAAF Wirraways did their own fly-under. These days tourists and locals love climbing it. I've made the Bridge Climb three times. By day, at twilight, and by night."

"It can't be for the faint-hearted?"

"Well, there are safety precautions, of course. One has to give a blood-alcohol reading, for a start. Then there's the Climb Simulator, to get an idea of what one might experience. But the view is worth it a million times over. It's absolutely breathtaking."

"Like now!" she replied. "Christopher would find this the most marvellous adventure."

"He'll see it." Rohan spoke matter-of-factly. He might have issues with her, but he had bonded with his son on sight. Such was the power of blood.

A company limo was standing by to take them the short distance to her city hotel, beautifully positioned between the Opera House and the Harbour Bridge. She had insisted on checking into a hotel, even though she knew she would be spending the night with Rohan at his Harbourside apartment. That was their agreement. But she had promised Christopher she would ring him from her hotel when she arrived, and tell him of all the excitement of the helicopter flight. Plus there was the fact she wanted to offer at least token resistance to Rohan's command of events.

He accompanied her to her luxurious room, looking around him as if to assure himself everything was up to scratch. "You know as well as I do, Rohan, this hotel has a reputation for excellence," she protested mildly. "But I suppose as you've paid for it you're entitled to check out the mod-cons."

"Thank you for thinking of that, Charlotte," he returned suavely. "I have a little trip planned for us this afternoon after lunch."

"It can't top the flight. That was wonderful. I'm going to ring Chrissie in a minute. He's the main man in my life."

"He's now the main man in *my* life as well. What I have in mind, my beautiful Charlotte, is to take you on a visit to my mother."

She was taken by complete surprise.

"Remember, I do have one?" he said, sardonically. "One of these days I might even go in search of my father."

She slumped onto the bed, staring up at him. "Have you found out who he is? Your mother told you?"

"Miraculously, *yes*. A huge step for mankind. She

hadn't told a soul—including the grandmother who reared her—but…"

"But, what?"

He lowered his lean length into an armchair, facing her. "I'm surprised you haven't guessed, Charlotte. You were always so intuitive. I was in rather a mess when I found out you'd married Martyn. But that was nothing to finding out you'd borne him a child. My mother was very worried about me. She decided at long last she was going to tell me what had happened to her when she was very young."

"Are you going to share it with me?"

Tension snapped and hummed as if overhead electricity wires were strung across the room.

"Why not? My father is Italian. Who would have thought it? I had always assumed he was Australian. But my birth father was born and lived in Rome. He and a few of his well-heeled student friends were tripping around the world, enjoying a university vacation. The Opera House, apparently, was a must-see for him. He was an architectural student, and the Opera House is a magnet for architects as well as millions of people from around the world. It was Jorn Utzon's *tour de force*, after all. He met my mother while the two of them were wandering around the plateau. He was taking photographs for his own records. They got to talking. That was the start of it! He was something of a polyglot, which no doubt helped. Apparently he spoke fluent English, French—and Italian, of course. My mother thought him the most fascinating human being she had ever met in her life. She fell for him hook, line and sinker. Whether he was just taking advantage of a pretty girl in a foreign country, I don't know. She says *not*. But she knew their romance couldn't last. Too much against it. He was from another country and a totally different background, obviously wealthy."

"Yet she took enormous risks?"

"A lot of us make mistakes when we're young, Charlotte," he said dryly. "I don't have to tell *you* that. He swore he would write to her, but he never did. Once he was home again among his own people his holiday romance would soon have faded away. Happens all the time." He gave a cynical shrug.

"But you know his name?"

There was a slight flare to his nostrils. He looked every inch a man of high mettle. "I do. He's most likely married, with grown-up children. He wouldn't be all that happy to discover he'd left an illegitimate son in far-off Australia. It would upset the apple cart. No, Charlotte, I'm the product of a short, sweet encounter. Maybe he remembers my mother now and again. She must have been very pretty. She still is."

"I believe it!" Very pretty, with lovely Celtic colouring that hadn't got a look-in with Christopher. "You're upset, Rohan?"

"Am I not supposed to be?" he challenged. "You're so good at analysing people, Charlotte."

"I'm good at analysing *you*," she returned with some spirit. "Don't be bitter."

"My dear Charlotte, I'm *managing* my bitterness. You know, in some ways you and my mother are alike. Both of you have lived your lives withholding vital information. Both of you took it upon yourselves to decide the outcome of your pregnancies. My mother told no one. You decided to go with a great lie."

She flushed at the hardness of the gaze. "So you're going to take it out on me for ever?"

"No. Let's forget about it." He rose lithely to his feet. "Worse things have happened at sea. I have a couple of things I need to attend to. I'll pick you up in an hour.

Remember me to my son, won't you? Tell him I'll organise another trip for him. His friend Peter too, if he likes. Mattie always thought of me whenever there was a trip on offer."

"Mattie worshipped you."

He sighed deeply. "Matthew should have been allowed to run wild when we were kids, but your mother insisted on cooping him up. I find that truly sad."

Neither of them spoke for a moment, both lost in the past. Charlotte was the first to recover. "I must tell you something that now appears not all that amazing. Christopher says he wants to be an architect when he grows up. He's seen the Opera House many times. We've been out on the Harbour. He thinks the sails are like the rising waves of the Pacific. He used to draw them over and over, lamenting he could never get them right. Dad's been happy to buy books for him. He's told him all about the brilliant young Danish architect who had no computer to work with, no internet, just a drawing board. Christopher is very good at art. His skills are way beyond his peers, according to his art teacher."

"Good grief!" Rohan looked surprised. "I can draw myself. You'll remember that? But these days we have all the technology we need to hand. I never thought of becoming an architect, even if we'd had the money. But *Christopher*!"

"I guess blood will out," she said quietly.

"Then we have to see he realises his dream." Rohan turned brisk. "We'll have lunch, then we'll go and see my mother. I bought her a very nice apartment at Point Piper." He named one of the most sought-after areas to live in Sydney. "It has everything going for it. The best north-facing Harbour views, easy access to the city, exclusive shops and restaurants, ocean beaches nearby."

She caught him up at the door, laying a detaining hand on his arm. "Does she know about Christopher?" Her green eyes were huge with concern.

"Don't panic," he said quietly. "She *would* if she ever laid eyes on him. But no, Charlotte, I'm not cruel. My mother knows I've bought Riverbend. She knows I went after *you*, seeing as I don't seem capable of staying away," he said with a degree of self-contempt. "And I've told her we're back together again."

"What did she say to that?" Her expression grew more anxious.

His strong arms encircled her waist as he drew her to him. He dropped a light kiss on her mouth—not soft, but subtle—lingering over it as though there were no better way for the two of them to communicate. "What makes me happy makes my mother happy," he said when he lifted his head.

"But she knows how much I hurt you. She must know that I…" Her voice faltered, gave out.

"Unquestionably it will be a great shock to her to find out Christopher is *my* son, not Martyn Prescott's. But you can be sure of one thing. She will welcome Christopher, her *grandson*, with open arms."

"If not me?" There was great sadness and regret in her tone. Mary Rose of the flame-coloured hair had adored her son, her only child. She would feel very strongly about what had been done to him to this day.

"Lucky for you, my mother has a very loving heart, Charlotte. A great blessing when *your* mother gave herself up to obsession."

"She didn't know how to control it!" she responded, with a show of heat. "She didn't know how to properly *love*! She's not the only one."

"Indeed she isn't." He dropped his encircling arms, his face grim. "Some of it must have rubbed off on you."

She swung away, her body quaking with nerves. Once she had been a very spirited young person—full of life, full of a bright challenge. But all the stuffing had been knocked out of her. "I'm having second thoughts about staying, Rohan," she warned him.

He glanced very casually at his handsome gold watch. "I'll pick you up in the foyer. We might as well have lunch here. The restaurants are very good. Then on to my mother's. All that has happened you'll find she'll forgive you, Charlotte. After all, like you, she's a woman with a past."

"The last word as ever, Rohan?" she countered.

He spun back, his low laugh sardonic. "It was *you* who had the last word, Charlotte. But times have changed." He reached only a few inches to pull her back into his arms. "What about letting yourself go for a minute?" he challenged, his blue eyes alight. "See it as practice, if you like. *Kiss me, Charlotte.* The sort of kiss that will carry me right through the day." His hands slid gently down her shoulders. "Remember how we used to sleep together naked, our limbs entwined? My arms around the silky curves of your body. The scent of your skin was wonderful! Peaches and citrus and something subtly musky too. God, how I loved you! I could never get enough of you. So kiss me, Charlotte. It's a simple thing."

Only it wasn't simple at all. It was as terrifying as taking a leap off the edge of a cliff. She *wanted* to kiss him. Kiss him deeply. She wanted to hold his dark head with her hands. She wanted to express her profound sense of loss and grief. In the end she lifted herself onto her toes, touching her lips to his. It was a feather-light kiss, so gentle, her hand caressing the side of his face. His darkly olive skin had a faint rasp from his beard.

He opened his mouth slightly to accommodate her. Immediately she slipped the tip of her tongue into the cavity, brushing it over his fine white teeth and the inside of his upper lip. He tasted wonderful. Her body was reacting very strongly. The kiss deepened into something *real*. The fever of it, the never-to-be-forgotten rapture... The time they had *wasted*!

His hand slid down the creamy column of her neck, pale as a rose, closing on the small high mound of her breast. The sensitive coral-pink nipple was already erect, like a tiny budding fruit.

"Is this kiss *real*?" he drew back a little to ask. To taunt? "It seems real to me."

"Rohan, don't let's fight. I only want us to become closer."

"Well, we do have tonight." His handsome head descended and he began to kiss in earnest. So deeply, so ravenously, that after a while she fully expected both of them would simply topple to the floor, captives of passion.

It was beautiful. It was agonising. It was a language both of them spoke perfectly...

Then suddenly his hands on her shoulders were firm. He was holding her away, male supremacy absolute. "Some things can't be crushed, can they?" he muttered ironically. "It's the same as it used to be, our lovemaking."

"You sound like it's a curse." She could barely speak for the thudding of her heart and the turmoil in her flesh.

"Some curse!" he said with a twisted smile. He dropped his hands, becoming businesslike. "I'm sure you've brought a dress to wear this afternoon. Not that I don't love the jeans and T-shirt. You have a great body. But a dress, I think. I'm sure my mother will agree you're even more beautiful now than you were as a girl. God knows, your grace and beauty turned me inside out."

Charlotte touched him with a trembling hand. "Let's try to be kind to one another, Rohan."

He thought that over for a tense moment, then flashed his white smile. Their son's smile. "Why not? For old times' sake, if nothing else."

They were actually outside the door of Mary Rose Costello's luxury apartment. Charlotte was in a daze of apprehension, trying to grapple with the speed of recent events. The force of her beating heart was stirring the printed silk of her dress. She was seeking forgiveness, but she didn't know how she could begin to deserve it. She wasn't the only one haunted by the events of the past. So was Rohan—and his mother. If Mary Rose Costello even suspected she had a little grandson who had been denied to her...

Dear God!

Rohan took her hand, his long fingers twining with hers. "Just like the old days," he said sardonically, standing back a little as his mother opened the door to them. Her expression was composed, but it had to be said a shade austere.

Charlotte just escaped making some little exclamation. Mary Rose Costello, a woman well over forty, looked a good ten years younger—as pretty and polished a woman as one could hope to see. Her former shock of copper-red hair was cut short and beautifully styled. Her complexion was the genuine redhead's classic alabaster. Not a wrinkle in sight. She looked rich and cared for down to her pearly fingertips. Petite and slight as ever, she was wearing a lovely cool maxi-dress—white splashed with small flowers.

Mary Rose Costello looked back at Charlotte keenly. There was no welcoming smile on her face. No big hello. *Maybe she might flatly refuse to let me in?* Charlotte agonised, worried her treacherous knees might buckle. Maybe Mary Rose would start to vent her stored-up rage? Charlotte half expected it. Perhaps would have *preferred* rage to a false welcome. Still, she made the first move.

"Mrs Costello." She held out her hand. "I only learned from Rohan of this visit today. You don't have to ask me in if you don't want to." She wasn't going to cry, but she felt very much like it. Instead she bit the inside of her lip.

Mary Rose took a few seconds to respond. "You and my son have reunited, Charlotte. It's only natural I should agree to his request to invite you." A moment's hesitation, then she stepped forward, drawing the taller Charlotte into a short hug. "Come in, my dear. You must remember I was always very fond of you."

"I'm so grateful, Mrs Costello." Charlotte didn't look back at Rohan.

"My son looks after me in style, as you can see." Mary Rose flashed a proud loving smile in Rohan's direction. "But I do own and run a successful boutique in Double Bay. I was always very interested in fashion, if you remember? I'll show you over the boutique one day soon."

"Thank you. I'd be interested to see it. I remember all the lovely dresses you used to make." She was in peril of mentioning her mother, who had been so good and then so very vengeful towards the Costellos. She was feeling unreal. It was getting to be a constant state of mind.

"Come along, darling," Rohan said with the greatest show of affection, taking hold of Charlotte's nerveless arm and guiding her into the living room.

All for his mother's benefit, of course. Charlotte was fully conscious of that. They needed to present a united front. This was the first step. The more difficult ones were to follow.

"Please do call me Mary Rose, Charlotte." Mary Rose

indicated they should both take a seat on one of the richly textured cream sofas. The seats were separated by a long black lacquer coffee table holding several coffee table books and an exquisite arrangement of pure white hippeastrum heads, packed into a simple but elegantly-shaped white porcelain vase.

"How very beautiful!" Charlotte remarked, loving the purity of the arrangement.

"We have a wonderful young florist in the area, fast becoming known." Mary Rose had expected Charlotte to notice. "She really brings the beauty of even a few flowers to life. I must show you her beautiful white butterfly orchid in a pot. She put the pot into a bed of bright green moss inside a glass vase like a large tumbler. I love white flowers."

"As do I." Charlotte looked around the living room, grateful for a little breathing space. How did one go about having a conversation when all the important issues had to be avoided like the plague? The living room was spacious, and elegantly decorated, with many imaginative touches and a small collection of very fine art. "I recognise the work of that artist," she said, naming a painter famous for her abstracts. One of her large canvases hung above the white marble mantel—dramatic, but beautifully calm.

"Rohan bought it for my birthday," Mary Rose said, with the sweetest smile she reserved for her son.

How would she smile at her grandson? *Would* she smile?

"It makes a balance for the panoramic views, don't you think, Charlotte?" Rohan was acting lover-like to the hilt. "I had a landscaper come in to make a little green oasis on the balcony."

"What I can see of it is stunning." Small-talk was going a little way to helping her relax. Through the open sliding glass doors she could see many beautiful plants growing in planter troughs. An eye-catching green flowering wall had been integrated into the design.

"My lovely lush sanctuary." Mary Rose smiled. "It's amazing what they're doing these days with apartment balconies. You look very beautiful, Charlotte." Mary Rose took a seat on the opposite sofa.

"Thank you." Charlotte responded quietly. She had never been comfortable with comments on her physical beauty. It was all in the genes anyway. There were many other things besides regular features.

"The last thing Charlotte is is vain." Rohan caught Charlotte's hand, carrying it to his mouth. He did it so beautifully he might well have meant it. Only they were putting on a show for his mother.

"May I say how wonderful *you* look?" Charlotte offered, in a sincere compliment. She didn't dare withdraw her hand from Rohan's. No telling what he might do next.

"I have to admit to a little hard work. I go to a gym twice a week. My son likes me to look my best. And of course I have to look good for the boutique. My clients expect it."

"Not a lot look as good or as youthful as my mother," Rohan said.

"That I well believe."

Was it going to be this simple? Charlotte thought. On the face of it she appeared to be accepted and forgiven. But then Mary Rose didn't know she had been deprived of her grandson—shut out of his early life, the precious infant and toddler years.

Inevitably the conversation, just as she'd dreaded, had to come around to Martyn. "I was very sorry to hear of his premature death." Mary Rose's face contorted slightly. "He was your husband. It must have been awful for you and for little Christopher. Rohan has told me what a remarkable little boy he is. Would you have a photo with you? If so, I'd love to see it."

Heart hammering, Charlotte opened her handbag, taking out her wallet. She had been meaning to replace the small photo of Christopher at age five with a current one. Now she was glad she hadn't. Christopher's blond curls clustered around his head. He was smiling. He looked like an angel. "This was taken a couple of years ago," she said, removing the photograph and handing it across to Mary Rose—her son's paternal grandmother.

Mary Rose started forward to take it. Her gaze rested on it for quite a while, then she lifted her copper head slowly. "You won't believe this, but he looks a bit like my Rohan when he was younger. Rohan didn't start out with dark hair, you know. It was fair for a few of those early years. Of course your boy has inherited the Marsdon blond hair," Mary Rose said, retaining her searching expression. "He's as beautiful as you are. He must be a great joy to you. But I can't see he looks much like you at this stage, Charlotte. Or Martyn." She frowned.

"He keeps changing." Charlotte felt the pulse beating in her temple.

"I must meet him." Mary Rose handed the photo back. "And your mother and father? How are they?"

"Didn't Rohan tell you?" Charlotte turned her head to look into Rohan's fire-blue eyes.

Rohan didn't answer. He waited for his mother's response.

Mary Rose shook her head. "I never really wanted to go there, Charlotte," she said. "Those years after you lost your brother and my son lost his dearest friend were very hard on all of us. The way my son was blamed by your mother broke my heart. But as a mother I understood she was out of her mind with grief. Still, it was a very painful time. Thank God my son has moved on. So have I. And here you are again, back in my son's life—as I often felt you would be, despite all the odds. Rohan tells me you and he are planning to get married very soon?"

She fixed her hazel gaze on Charlotte's face, with no attempt at lightness. This was the young woman who had broken her beloved son's heart. She had rejected him so she could have it all. Or so it had seemed. But even then, Mary Rose realised, some part of her had questioned Charlotte's motivation. Charlotte Marsdon had never been one to cause pain. The daughter of privilege, she had always been her lovely graceful self with everyone. Social standing hadn't come into it.

"Yes." Charlotte sat, her slender body taut, a whole weight of emotion in her eyes. "I want you to forgive me, Mrs Costello—Mary Rose. We need your blessing. *I* need your blessing. Finally I get to do the right thing." She stopped before she burst into tears.

"Then you *have* my blessing." Mary Rose Costello was herself holding back tears. "You need to get a life for yourself, Charlotte. For yourself and for your son. It's terrible, the loss of all the good years. Take it from someone who knows."

CHAPTER SEVEN

CHARLOTTE recognised any number of people as she entered the huge function room on Rohan's arm. From somewhere a small orchestra was playing classical music. It was barely audible above the loud hum of conversation and laughter. The glassed-in walls, the lighting, the profusion of flowers and green plants, the women's beautiful evening dresses all lent the grand ballroom of one of Sydney's most glamorous venues for social and charity events an exotic look—rather like a splendid conservatory. Tonight's function was to raise funds for a children's leukaemia foundation, and there was a heart warming turnout.

Many people had marked their arrival. She was aware that heads were turning in all directions.

"Ah, there's Charlotte Prescott back on the scene. You remember her husband? A bit of a scandal there. And isn't that the new mover and shaker she's with? Rohan Costello?"

Charlotte acknowledged the people she knew with a little wave and a smile. Her mother had been a great fundraiser.

A woman's face stood out in the crowd—if only because of the cold distaste of her expression and the rigidity in the set of her head and shoulders. It was Diane Rodgers, looking very elegant in black and silver. Her dark eyes

focused quite alarmingly on Charlotte and then moved
on to Rohan. But Rohan had his head turned go the side,
saluting a colleague.

Thank God Ms Rodgers wasn't seated at their table,
Charlotte thought, wondering if Rohan had anything to do
with it. Diane Rodgers was an assertive go-getter. It was
painfully obvious she had convinced herself she had a real
chance with Rohan, and her bitter disappointment over
the destruction of her daydreams had turned to loathing
of her perceived rival. Unrequited love could be a terrible
business.

Rohan knew everyone at their table, and swiftly and charm-
ingly made introductions. Charlotte was greeted warmly.
Waiters appeared with champagne. The evening was
underway.

Charlotte gazed around her with pleasure. The ballroom, which had one of the most spectacular views of
Sydney Harbour, was a glitter of lights. The circular tables
placed all around the huge room had floor-length cloths
of alternating pastel blue, pink and silver. The chairs were
tied with broad bands of silver satin. Small arrangements
of blue hydrangeas or posies of pink roses acted as cen-
trepieces. Massed clouds of pink, blue and silver balloons
were suspended from the ceiling. The huge screen up on
the dais showed the logo of the charity in the familiar
colours.

Guests had really dressed up for the occasion. Men
in black tie, women wearing the sorts of gowns one saw
flipping over the pages of *Vogue*. Everyone had the sense
this was going to be a most successful evening, for a very
deserving charity. Charlotte was pleased to see some of
the richest and most powerful men in the country seated

at tables not far from them. That could only mean a great deal of money would be raised.

Hours later, after a very successful evening, it was time to go home. Just as Charlotte had expected, Diane Rodgers, dark eyes glowing like coals, was lying in wait for Rohan.

"Won't be a moment," Rohan told Charlotte with a wry smile.

"That's okay."

A beaming, portly elderly man was making for Charlotte, calling her name in a delighted voice. Charlotte held out her hand to ex-senator Sir Malcolm Fielding. "How lovely to see you, Malcolm." She held up her cheek for his kiss. Malcolm Fielding had gone to school and university with her grandfather. They had always remained good friends. In the old days Malcolm and his late wife had been frequent visitors to Riverbend.

"Your mother is here, dear—did you know?" Malcolm Fielding looked about, as though trying to locate Barbara in the moving throng.

"No, I didn't," Charlotte answered, calmly enough, though her feelings were rapidly turning to blind panic. *Her mother!* She was lucky if her mother ever answered one of her calls.

"An impressive lady, your mother," said Malcolm. "And still a handsome woman. A bit chilly though, dear. Even her smile, wouldn't you say? Terrible tragedy about young Mattie, but Barbara might be reminded she still has *you*. I was totally blitzed when your parents separated. But tragedy can sometimes do that to people."

He looked over Charlotte's shining blonde head. "Oh—a bit early, but there's my ride!" he exclaimed. "Can't keep them waiting. A flawless event, wouldn't you say, Charlotte? All the more because we met up." He kissed her cheek again. "I couldn't help noticing the young man you're with," he added roguishly. "Costello is making quite a name for himself. No relation to our ex-treasurer. Don't forget to remember me to your father, now. Tell him to give me a ring. We'll have lunch at the club."

"Will do, Sir Malcolm." Charlotte smiled, although a feeling of alarm was invading her entire body. Had her mother seen her with Rohan? Why was she so surprised her mother was in Sydney? She had spotted many a Melbournite who had flown in to attend this big charity function.

To calm her agitation she started walking along with the happy, chattering crowd towards one of the arched doorways that led onto the street. She knew Rohan would follow fairly soon. Outside, limousines were starting to cruise, picking up their passengers. The headlights picked up the multi colours of the women's dresses and the brilliance of their jewellery.

Charlotte was just slowing her steps so she wouldn't get too far ahead of Rohan when a woman's firm hand caught her from behind.

"One moment, Charlotte."

Charlotte turned back to face her mother.

I'm scared of this woman, she thought. *Scared of my own mother. Or of the bitter, backward-looking woman my mother had become.*

She wanted to run, but knew she had to stand her ground. "Good evening, Mother," she said courteously. "Is Kurt with you?" Kurt Reiner was a decent enough man. Very rich, of course.

"Forget Kurt!" Barbara Reiner snapped explosively. "He's somewhere. At the moment I don't give a toss where." Barbara Reiner's haughty face with its classic features had become marred over the years by a perpetual expression of malcontent.

"I didn't see you. It was such a big turn-out. Malcolm Fielding told me you were here. You look very well." Her mother wore vintage Dior, black lace, with a double string of South Sea pearls around her throat and large pearl pendant drops.

"The emeralds, I see!" She showed bitter disappointment that they weren't hanging from her own neck.

"Dad gave me permission to wear them."

"Well, he would, wouldn't he? He always did indulge you." Barbara's narrowed glance darted back to where Rohan was standing with the Premier and his wife. They were about to enter the back seat of a Rolls-Royce. "Tell me that's not Rohan Costello?" Fury streaked across Barbara's cold, distinguished face.

"Why ask a question when you know the answer?" Charlotte replied quietly. "You know perfectly well it's Rohan. Does anyone else look like him? Besides, you must have taken note of his very generous donation."

"So he's done well for himself." Barbara gritted her teeth. "He's got himself a *life*. Unlike my dead boy."

They would never rise above their family tragedy. "Nothing but Mattie. Nothing but Mattie," Charlotte moaned. "It's about time you pulled out of your tortured state of mind, Mum. Matthew would never have wanted it."

Barbara lifted a hand as though about to strike. "Don't you *ever* tell me how to live my life, Charlotte. I will mourn my son until the day I die. The agony will never go away."

"I understand that, Mum." Charlotte hastened to placate her. "But Dad and I grieve too. We loved Mattie."

"No one grieves like a mother," Barbara shot back.

"What would you do if you lost your boy? Go on—tell me. Losing a child is the worst blow a woman can ever suffer in life."

"You don't have to tell me that, Mum. I adore my son. But I can never forget that you once told me it was a pity it wasn't me who'd drowned instead of Mattie." Charlotte gave her mother a look of incurable hurt. "You don't have any deep regrets over that? You'd have got over *my* death, wouldn't you? Probably completely. Please let go of my arm."

Barbara had the grace to comply. "I've only just heard Costello was behind the purchase of Riverbend." She said it as though a monstrous deal had been done.

Charlotte began to walk away from the crowd. Quite a few people had been looking their way. Her mother was forced to follow. The breeze off the water caught at Charlotte's long blonde hair and the hem of her exquisite white chiffon gown. "Please keep your voice down, Mum. It's very carrying."

"Of course it is. Clarity and resonance has stood me in good stead. What I really feel like doing is scream-ing my head off." Barbara was visibly struggling for self-possession. "You're back with him, of course. The boy's his, isn't he? Your father might be a fool, but you can't fool me, Charlotte. I've always had my suspicions. You were pregnant by Costello, yet you married poor Martyn. What a terrible injustice! Did you ever get around to telling him his son was really Rohan Costello's child?" Barbara's demeanour showed frightening aggression.

"No, I didn't. Never!" It was hard to maintain control. "It might shock you, but I believed when I married Martyn he *was* the father of my child."

"I didn't come down in the last shower!" Barbara gave a contemptuous laugh. "You chose to marry *money*,

Charlotte. I understand that at least. Only a foolish woman thinks she can live on love alone—or what passes for love. A driving lust was all you had for Costello."

"Lust?" Charlotte was compelled to swallow down her anger. "What *is* to become of you, Mum? You're deeply neurotic. You need help."

Even in the semi-dark it was possible to see Barbara's flush. "Don't go too far, my girl," she warned. "What would have happened had your husband lived?" There was challenge in her voice. "When you think about it, you were cheating on both of them. Fancy that! Your father's saintly *angel,* with her long blonde hair, having sex with two young men at the same time. I can only marvel!"

"Marvel away!" Charlotte invited, chilled to the bone though the night was warm. She leaned in close to her mother. "I didn't have sex with Martyn, Mum. He *forced* sex on me." It was a measure of her upset that she revealed what she had never revealed before.

Her mother, who had been glaring at her, drew back with a fierce bark of laughter. "I—don't—believe—you."

"Why not, when you're so smart?" Charlotte was close to despair. She had just confided what she'd thought wild horses wouldn't drag out of her. "Things got out of hand. I begged him to stop but he wouldn't. *Couldn't.* I had to live with him. So I learned to think of it that way."

"As well you might!" Barbara drew further back in disgust. "Martyn was totally in love with you, you little fool! It's clear to me you must have led him on," she raged. "You know what you are?"

"Do tell me." Charlotte stood fast. It seemed as if mother-daughter love had gone for ever.

Rohan, unnoticed by both of them, was now only a few feet away. "Charlotte!"

"Don't attempt to drag Rohan into this," Charlotte warned, able to gather herself now Rohan was returning.

"I can and I *will*," Barbara stated forcefully.

Charlotte's heart pumped double-time.

"Good evening, Mrs Reiner," Rohan said.

He looked the very image of a staggeringly handsome and highly successful young man about town, but Barbara stormed towards him as though he were a deadbeat. "You two deserve one another, you know. Do you think I'm a fool?"

Rohan answered with complete self-control. "I certainly don't think you're a fool, Mrs Reiner. So what's the point of acting like one? I'm sure you don't really want to draw attention to yourself. *You're* the one with the fine reputation, after all."

Barbara's coiffed head shot back. "Kindly treat me with respect, Costello," she said, with shocking arrogance.

"Maybe I'll do that when you do the same for me," Rohan replied suavely. He took Charlotte's trembling arm, aware of just how much punishment Charlotte had taken over the years. Barbara Marsdon had been unbelievably cruel to her daughter. "We'll say goodnight, Mrs Reiner. I see you've been giving Charlotte hell. Nothing new in that."

Barbara's stare was malignant. She took in his impressive height and physique, the way he held himself, the self-assuredness, the cultured voice, his stunning good-looks. And those *eyes*! Mary Rose Costello's illegitimate child had come a long way. There was no sign of remorse in him—no plea for forgiveness. Didn't he know Mattie's death had nearly killed her? There was no reality any more. No normal life. Sometimes she thought it would have been best had she drowned with her son. And to think Rohan Costello was back into their lives! He still wanted

her daughter! That couldn't be allowed. As for the boy...
A bitter resentment rolled off Barbara in waves.

"So confident," she said icily, as though he had no right
to be. "And haven't you grown inches? But you'll be hear-
ing more from me, Rohan Costello. That I can promise."

"Then please do keep it civil, Mrs Reiner." Rohan retained his low, even tone. "I wouldn't want to take action
against you."

Barbara didn't deign to answer. She turned away, trying
to get her ravaged face in order before she went back to
her husband. How she wished something horrible would
happen to Rohan Costello! So arrogant, so challenging, and
far, far too confident. As for her daughter! She was going
to reserve a little time and place for Charlotte...

"God, I think we could do with a couple of major tranquil-
lisers after that brush with your mother." Rohan put out his
hand to signal his approaching limousine driver. "What do
you suppose she knows about hiring hit men?"

"Don't laugh, Rohan." Charlotte's beautiful face was full
of upset. She was bitterly regretting her admission about
Martyn. She knew she would have to pay for it somewhere
down the line.

"So what do you want me to do? Buy a suit of armour?
Your mother ran out on you and your father. She should
not be allowed to interfere in your life. And she had better
consider that *your* life is *my* life."

CHAPTER EIGHT

THEY were inside Rohan's penthouse apartment up in the clouds within twenty minutes. This was the second time Charlotte had been inside. As she'd promised to stay overnight she'd left her suitcase there before they had gone on to the function.

"I'm going to pour myself a stiff Scotch." Rohan reached a hand to a bank of switches. "What about you?"

He looked back at her. She looked supremely beautiful, but with a *fragile* overlay that didn't surprise him. He felt rattled himself. Some women were born martyrs. Barbara Marsdon-Reiner was one of them. The incredible thing was that in the pre-Mattie Tragedy days Barbara had been a nice woman. Obviously her whole mode of thinking had altered drastically after the terrible experience of losing her son. Her loathing of *him* hadn't gone away. It still held sway.

"I'll have a brandy." It was all Charlotte could think of. "A good French cognac, if you've got it."

"Which one of them *isn't* good?" he asked with a touch of humour.

They moved through the entrance hall with its stunning gold and white marble floor. An important seascape hung above an antique black and gold commode. The large living room beyond matched up with the hall in its refined opulence. Very European.

"Go sit down while I take a look." He walked away to a well-stocked drinks trolley, with an assortment of crystal decanters, and bent over it, checking. "You're in luck. I've the best of the best Hennessy and a Rémy Martin. One or the other should do the trick. Both nearly sent me broke."

"The Rémy Martin." Her father's choice. Budgeting, so far as her father was concerned, didn't include fine wines and brandies.

She felt shot through with desolation. The awful way her mother had attacked Rohan! Unforgivable. By her mother's lights Rohan Costello should have been one great big failure in life. Instead he had made an outstanding success of himself.

Unable to settle, she drifted about the living room. "If I hadn't thought it before, I think grief has unhinged my mother," she offered sadly.

"You only *think*?" Rohan's dark head lifted. "Did she seem dangerous to you?" He wasn't entirely joking.

"Oh, don't say that!" She gave an involuntary shudder.

"Then what would you say?"

"Dad's lucky to be out of it?" She managed a wry laugh.

"You bet he is." Rohan continued fixing their drinks, fighting down the powerful urge to simply go to her, sweep her up in his arms and carry her into the bedroom.

How many times had Martyn Prescott swept her up in his arms? Hundreds? He couldn't bear to think about it. Not now.

"*You're* lucky too," he said. "And don't let me start on how lucky our son is. It's a good thing Grandmama doesn't want to see him. You'd have to think very seriously about that, Charlotte. I sure do. After tonight I wouldn't want her around him. Up until your mother's appearance it had been a brilliant night. We didn't really need her to mess it up."

She sighed deeply, turning to face the floor-to-ceiling sliding glass doors. The apartment had stupendous views of the Harbour and city on three sides. Glorious by day, it was absolutely breath-taking by night. A wonderland of glittering multi-coloured lights. This was very much a *man's* apartment. It had the feel of an exclusive gentlemen's club. She ran her hands appreciatively over the back of a black leather armchair. A custom-built sofa nearby was upholstered in a knobbly black and gold fabric of striking design. So easily did Rohan fit into these luxurious surroundings they might have been his heritage.

"My mother is one of the despairs of my life." She sank into the sofa. "She defeats me. I've loved her throughout all our traumas, but I can no longer cope. My mother still hates you. Can you believe it?"

"Charlotte, do please pay attention. Some old hatreds never die. Let's forget about your dear mother. I have it in my heart to spare a thought for poor old Reiner. He can't be a happy man."

"Maybe he drinks himself into oblivion when Mum sinks into one of her moods."

Rohan had to laugh, though he was deeply affected by the sadness in her face. Charlotte's *blondeness* and the pure white chiffon of her dress made her a vision of femininity against the lushly dark background of his sofa. She was removing the glorious Marsdon diamond and emerald earrings, putting them down on the coffee table. He watched her shake out her hair.

"Lord, those earrings are heavy," she sighed. "So is the necklace."

"Leave it," Rohan ordered, as she put up her hands to the clasp.

Adrenalin made a mad rush into her veins. "Why? Have you something erotic in mind?'

"Haven't *you*?" His blue eyes glittered. "We're so good at it."

"Old history, Rohan."

"Really?" His handsome mouth curled. Her cool touch-me-not look was incredibly sexy. "You still enjoy being kissed." He handed over a crystal brandy balloon, containing a good shot of cognac. "There's the same old excitement."

"So why don't *you* feel better about the whole thing?"

He didn't answer. Her beauty made its own light, he thought. She didn't need diamonds and emeralds. "I'll feel better when I know the whole story," he said eventually. "Mind if I sit beside you?"

"Oh, Rohan!" She was searingly aware of the devilment in his eyes.

"Relax, Charlotte." Instead he took an armchair. He had undone his black tie, letting it dangle against the snow-white of his dress shirt. He looked like a man one could only dream about.

"I love where you live." She took a slow sip of the cognac, feeling the subtle fire.

He flicked a careless glance around the living room. "It cost a good deal of money. But I'm happy with it."

"So how much time are you going to be able to spend at Riverbend?" She fixed her gaze on the contents of her brandy balloon as though it contained the answer. "Is it your intention to instal me there with Christopher?" Her eyes swept up to study him. The slant of a downlight gilded the planes and angles of his arresting face. Her heart turned

over with the endless love she couldn't find the courage
to put voice to.

"You mean do I intend to instal my wife and son there?"
he asked dryly. "The answer is yes. *I* have no heritage.
No background I can speak of. My biological father is a
mystery man. He has played no part in my life. My mother
and my grandmother had nothing. Mum had to work hard
to survive. I was smart enough to gain scholarships and
bursaries to secure my education. I want Christopher to
retain his Marsdon heritage."

"Only *you* have made it possible," she told him qui-
etly. "Life is very strange. Matthew should have inherited
Riverbend. And his children, had he lived to have them.
Now you say my son—"

"*Our* son," he corrected firmly.

"Will inherit?"

"Isn't that a comfort, Charlotte?" There was a tautness
in his voice.

"Beyond comfort, Rohan. My poor father raced through
his inheritance. I think he still doesn't quite know how it
happened. Losing Mattie blighted all our lives. But Dad
would have continued to make his ill-advised investments
even if Mattie had lived. So in the end Mattie would still
have missed out."

"I'm certain Matthew would have approved of his little
nephew as heir."

"He would." Charlotte was assailed by what might have
been. "Mattie would have loved him."

"Mattie would have given his life for you, Charlotte.
You were very close. I never heard a cross word pass between you. Yet you used to tell Martyn off left, right and
centre."

"He deserved it." Charlotte curled her fingers tightly

around her crystal glass. "It only takes one tragedy to affect so many other lives."

"Undoubtedly—but it doesn't come close to explaining how you came to choose Martyn over me. Every teacher, every tutor, all my classmates voted me the one most destined to succeed. You know. You were there. All I needed was a little time. As it turned out, *very* little time. I hit on a huge money-maker. It wasn't going to be my be-all and end-all. No way! But my every thought was for *you*, for our future together."

"Not all dreams have happy endings, Rohan," she said with a melancholy expression.

How could she ever tell Rohan that Martyn, their friend from childhood, had raped her? Such a hideous word she hesitated to think it, let alone give it voice. It was all too degrading. Rohan would be speechless with anger—some of which would have to fall on her for having given Martyn opportunity.

"Even now, my mother will do her utmost to break us up," she added.

"She won't succeed," he said, with absolute belief in himself. "I'm thinking an April wedding. We'll honeymoon in the European spring. Five months will give you time to get back into practice for loving me. It's a lifetime when a man wants a woman as desperately as I want you. You led me down the garden path, Charlotte, from when we were kids. We might not get the happy ending we talked about, but we do get another chance. We'll be together with our son."

She should have told him there and then that he was all she had ever wanted. Why didn't she? What was stopping her from saying, *Rohan, I love you. I've never stopped loving you. I was in despair when I had to marry Martyn. I truly believed I was carrying his child.* But she knew

Rohan's mind was focused on very different reasons. Getting back what he had once had was all that mattered to him now.

"What are you thinking about?" Rohan's voice brought her out of her reverie.

Her poignant smile tore at his heart.

All the awful stuff locked up inside her. The years with Martyn.

He'd *had* to have her. But oddly he'd never got her pregnant. She hadn't always taken precautions, believing she had a moral duty to give him his own child and his parents a *real* grandchild.

"I was thinking one has to pay for past sins," she said, bitter tears at the back of her throat.

"Not surprising, when the past is where it all began," he said quietly. "Come to bed."

The note in his voice, the look in his eyes, turned her limbs liquid. There was a *burning* along her veins. She didn't think she could move at all, or even draw breath, though her heart was soaring, lifting on wings.

Come to bed.

Could they really reclaim what they'd had? Passion was ravishing. Trust was something else again. Any relationship would flounder without trust.

"Finish your cognac if you think you need it."

She looked back at him across the space of seven years. The times they had been in each other's arms. The secret meetings. The secret language they'd used to communicate with one another. She thought of the passionate lovemaking, the delirious lovemaking, the soft, sweet lovemaking, of the times they'd been content to make each other laugh. They had been so *young*.

He had taken her virginity, himself a virgin. The first time for one had been the first time for the other. Only they had been quickly done with the kissing and the teasing. They had been driven to move on. Unfulfilled rapture was one thing, but there was too much physical pain involved if overwhelming desire couldn't find release.

How, then, could he believe for a moment she had sold herself to Martyn? How could he think her capable of such treachery? Shouldn't he be working his way through to some answers?

You're not helping him, chided the voice in her head.

How could she help him? My God, Martyn had done a job on her. She couldn't speak for the shame.

"Charlotte? Are you coming?" He held out his hand.

Her answer was little more than a whisper. She picked up her crystal balloon, took a last fevered gulp. Heat coursed down her throat, past her breasts into her stomach, then into the delta between her legs. That was where she wanted him—to make her cry out in rapture. She wanted other children. *His* children. Siblings for her darling Christopher.

He went to her, drawing her to her feet. Then his arms closed around her as if they were going to dance. Maybe he had some romantic ballad in his head? He must have, because he danced her around the quiet room, all the while staring down into her face.

She made an aching sound in her throat. There had been such heartbreak. But there was always *hope*. How could the intense love they had shared ever go entirely away? The space between them was throbbing with a sexual desire that had only picked up momentum.

"I want you so badly," he said, in an overpowering rush.

"*Want* is one word. Please tell me another."

"I *need* you." He kissed her cheek very softly.

"Can't you keep going?"

He was clasping her so tightly their bodies seemed

fused—his hard with desire. "What is it you want to hear? That I'll love you for ever and a day?"

"You used to tell me that." Her sadness was immense.

"The past is another country, Charlotte." He kissed the dip behind her ear.

"But you know how unpredictable life is." She lifted imploring green eyes. "Good things happen. Bad things happen. Life-altering things."

"We were supposed to face them together. I used to *dream* I would get you pregnant."

An incredible intimacy bonded them. "You *did*," she said softly.

"But you married Martyn."

"My mistake. I had to live with it." The opening was there again. A brave woman would have taken the hurdle. Only once more she balked. "Those years are over, Rohan. They were full of pain."

Frustration caught him by the throat. He wanted to shake the truth out of her. He had difficulty not doing it. "So why can't you *tell* me the whole story? Don't I have a right to know? Were you frightened of how your parents—your mother—would react? Knowing them, I can appreciate that. Was there *safety* and *security* in marrying Martyn? Pleasing your parents?"

Charlotte swallowed painfully. "Does it matter now?" The trouble was he was judging Martyn by his own standards. Martyn fell far below them. Martyn had been ill-equipped for not getting his own way, even by force. He had thought taking her was his right. Would the truth help her here?

"Okay. I'm done with talking."

Rohan's voice echoed his tension. He released her abruptly, so hard with desire he wanted to pull her down onto the rug and cover her there and then. His hunger was so strong. He wanted his body over hers. He wanted to forget those years when he'd thought his life had been smashed. If they had any chance at all he had to forget his bitterness, clamp down on his frustration. He had her now. He could so easily spoil things. Martyn had won her. But Martyn was gone.

She was a lightweight in his arms.

He carried her down the passageway to the master bedroom, cool from the air-conditioning. He let her body fall gently onto the luxurious bed. She bounced against its springiness before half rolling away from him.

He lowered himself onto the bed beside her, one hand on the slope of her bare shoulder, turning her back to him. "'While the one eludes, must the other pursue.' Browning, I think." He stared down into her river-green eyes. "I'm not looking for the right wife to live with, Charlotte. I've had other women. Nothing easy about being celibate. But I've never been able to wipe you out of my mind. Never lost my vivid memories of you. Attractive women came and *went*. All because of *you*. I found I didn't want a woman I could live happily enough with. I want a wife I can't live *without*. And that, Charlotte, is *you*. I know you never loved Martyn."

Her long hair glittered against the mix of gold, chocolate and black silk cushions that adorned the bed. That much she *could* admit. She *had* never loved Martyn.

"I'm trying so hard to understand."

"Then you'll use up all your understanding." Her defensive walls had been too long in place. "Make love to me, Rohan." She pressed a hand to her aching breast. "At least you *want* me."

"As you want me."

It was a statement not to be denied.

"Maybe we should let go of the past?" he suggested quietly.

"I want that too."

He turned her over, putting a hand to the long covered zipper on her evening dress. His nimble fingers unzipped her in one smooth movement before turning her back to him. "One thing, Charlotte." There was severity in his expression. "Never, *never* lie to me again."

A flush travelled all over her flawless skin. "I have never lied."

He dismissed that with a wave of his hand. "*Promise* me. Say it. *I'll never lie to you again, Rohan.*"

"Then you must say that to me too." Her eyes glowed as green as the ocean.

He didn't say a word. Neither did she.

Instead he began slowly to lower the bodice of her gown, revealing her small breasts, the white of roses. "Having our son hasn't changed your body," he said very quietly, his eyes gliding all over her as she lay on his bed. "Your breasts are still as perfect, the nipples coral-pink. See how they swell to my fingertips? Your waist is as narrow…" He began to peel the white chiffon dress further down her body like a man enthralled, listing his observations as he went. "Your stomach just as taut." He palmed his hand over it, circling and circling, moving lower, until he let his long fingers sink into the triangle of fine blonde hair at her core. "Remember all the crazy things we used to do?" His eyes were a perfect electric-blue. "Your body was my body. My body was yours. Two bodies. One beating heart. One soul."

She shivered to his touch. Beyond answering. She would picture how they'd been when she was dying. So young. Alone together. Without inhibition. Heat was sizzling up through her skin. Her whole body went into spasm as his fingers sought and then touched on an acutely sensitive spot. Her trembling legs fell apart. She wanted to lift them, wrap them around him, bind him to her. She wanted to make it up to him for every moment of those years of heartbreak.

His mouth came down on hers with a ravenous hunger, opening it up fully to his tongue. "Good," he muttered into the brandied sweet honey of her mouth. "Because we're going to do all of them again."

Love could bring either agony or ecstasy. Sometimes it brought both entwined.

The last time he had made love to her they had made a baby. A beautiful baby. Christopher.

Only she hadn't told him that momentous thing. It was beyond making sense of.

Within a week of that most memorable night Barbara Reiner decided it was high time to pay her daughter a visit. Vivian would most probably be at Riverbend—at the Lodge, of all places. Talk about a headlong fall from grace! Vivian was such a fool—always hiding his head in the sand. And to think he had sold the Marsdon ancestral home to Rohan Costello! It defied belief. But then Vivian was notorious for making horrendous decisions.

Silver Valley was only a few hundred miles from Sydney, but she certainly didn't intend to drive herself. She commandeered Kurt's Bentley and his chauffeur for the afternoon. Kurt had dared to rumble a tiny protest. Apparently he needed the car. But she had raised her eyebrows and told him to call a cab. She was looking forward to the trip. She knew Costello was in Sydney. She had rung his office, pretending she was a friend. No way did she want Costello anywhere on the scene. She didn't want him around to back up her daughter.

The boy would be at school. Rohan Costello's son. She could remember the precise moment when she'd first had her suspicions. She had been trying to give Charlotte some advice, and the boy—way too protective of his mother—had turned and given her such a piercing look of appraisal, with near-adult intelligence, she had been truly astonished. She had been judged and found wanting. It had suddenly dawned on her that she had seen that very look before. And those *brilliant blue eyes* didn't fit into the family, did they? Vivian had blue eyes, of course, but even as a young man they had never had that depth of colour, never mind the intensity of regard. She didn't actually *know*. She'd just had a gut feeling.

That was when she had started ignoring the boy. Others might find that extremely harsh, but they hadn't suffered like she had. And there was her daughter—the survivor. Charlotte hadn't learned her lesson. Costello was back in her life. There was going to be a scandal, but she had gone beyond caring. Anything to get back at Costello. He might have passed himself off in society, but his very humble beginnings were bound to come out. And there was the way poor Martyn had been treated! The only thing that would guarantee her silence was for Charlotte and Costello to split up. She presumed he didn't know the child was his. Any woman could pull the wool over a man's eyes. Men missed so much!

Charlotte couldn't remember the last time Christopher had had a day off school, but he—like a number of children and adults in the Valley—had caught a twenty-four-hour bug that had been doing the rounds. Mild enough, she had nevertheless decided to keep him at home for the day. Rohan had picked out some suitable computer games, so that would keep him occupied in his room.

It was a room any boy would envy. It housed his computer, a television, and a bookcase packed with a range of books on subjects that interested him. Not many boys Christopher's age shared his wide-ranging interest in learning and getting "the facts", but that was the way his mind worked. She had nearly fainted when his headmaster had made the chance remark, "The only other child I can remember as extraordinary as your boy, Mrs Prescott, was Rohan Costello."

One day Christopher would have to know the truth. But she recognised with gratitude that Rohan was as committed as she to giving their son time.

Christopher was actually the first to spot the Bentley sweeping up the driveway. It was after lunch. He ran back down the stairs, calling out excitedly to his mother, "Mummy, Mummy—I think maybe it's Grandmother in a Bentley."

Vivian Marsdon strode into the entrance hall. "Good God, surely not!"

"That will cost you, Grandpa!"

"Well, knock me down with a feather." Vivian changed tack, a huge frown on his face. "What do you suppose she wants?" he asked of his equally transfixed daughter.

"Maybe she's dropping in with goodies?" Christopher burst out laughing at his own joke.

Goodies, indeed. Charlotte felt only alarm. "Go back upstairs, darling. Stay in your room like a good boy."

"Can't I stay here?" Instinct told Christopher his mother and grandfather were preparing for trouble. They might need his help.

Vivian Marsdon confirmed his hunch. "There's something wrong with this. Why didn't she ring? I hope she hasn't got that b—husband of hers with her."

"Another fifty cents, Grandpa," Christopher reminded him, as the swear words started to come thick and fast.

"All right, all right. I'll pay up. Your mother is right. Go upstairs, Chrissie. Please don't come down until I come to get you."

Christopher took his mother's hand. "Won't it make you feel better if I stay? Grandmother doesn't worry me. She has no feelings for me."

Vivian Marsdon was aghast. "My dearest boy, your grandmother *loves* you. She just doesn't know how to show it."

Christopher gave his grandfather a kindly look. "It's okay, Grandpa. I don't miss her either."

"If I hadn't given up smoking I'd consider lighting up a cigar."

"Cigars are for celebration, aren't they?" Christopher asked.

"They're also an excellent way to soothe a man's nerves."

Charlotte smiled down on her son. "Do as I say, darling. Go back upstairs. Grandpa and I will take care of this."

Obediently Christopher turned away. "How do you know you can?" he paused to ask. "Grandmother is a serious pain in the a—"

"That will do, Christopher," Vivian Marsdon held up a warning hand. "I've told you not to use that crude expression."

"Sorry, Grandpa. By the way, she's by herself in the back seat. A chauffeur is driving. He's wearing a uniform with a hat."

"Dear Lord!" Vivian Marsdon rolled his eyes heavenward as Christopher disappeared up the stairs. "This is like waiting for a bomb to go off. Barbara has developed such a taste for doom and gloom, all she has left is her dark side."

Charlotte bowed her head in silent agreement. Her own concerns were intense. Today of all days, when Christopher was by chance home from school, her mother had arrived.

Barbara took tea before she launched into the reason for her unscheduled visit.

"It's about the boy," she said, setting down her fine bone-china cup.

"His name is Christopher," Vivian reminded his ex-wife testily. "The boy...the boy...I very much resent your calling your grandson that."

"So what do *you* call him?" Barbara asked, with a wild flash in her eyes.

Vivian stared back, utterly perplexed. "What on earth are you talking about, Barbara?"

Barbara's eyes shot to her daughter, who was looking very pale. "I see you haven't told your father?" she said, totally without sympathy.

"No one tells me a thing—how would I know?"

"Why are you doing this, Mum?" Charlotte asked. "Have you absolutely no compassion? No love in your heart?"

Barbara's tone was hard. "Don't try to turn the tables on me, Charlotte. I can't bear to be part of this...this... conspiracy," she cried, looking the very picture of self-righteousness.

Vivian Marsdon, provoked beyond measure, suddenly gave vent to a roar. "What the hell is this? Is it supposed to be some sort of trial, with you the judge and the jury, Barbara?"

She glared back at him. "Your golden angel betrayed us all," she said, riding a bitter wave. "She married poor

Martyn Prescott, knowing she was carrying Rohan Costello's child."

Vivian Marsdon's handsome face turned purple. *"W-h-a-t?"*

"Doesn't that make you feel good?" Barbara hurled at him. "Charlotte—your perfect girl—was having sex with both of them. She might have thought at the beginning it was Martyn's child—got her dates wrong—but it wouldn't have taken her long to wake up. The boy is enormously bright, I grant you. And poor Martyn was an idiot."

"You be very careful with what you're saying." Vivian Marsdon looked formidable. "If this is some vicious scheme from an old woman—"

"Old? *Old!*" For a moment Barbara looked as if she was going into cardiac arrest. "Why, you silly old man—I'm three years younger than you."

"And you're not looking good, Barbara. You're taking on the persona of the Wicked Witch of the West."

To Barbara it was a hard slap in the face. "For you of all people to say that! You loved me madly."

"And how much did you love *me*?" he countered, his mood abruptly shifting. "You never loved me, Barbara, did you? It was the Marsdon name. The Marsdon money."

Barbara gave him a vicious smile. "Which you promptly lost."

"Just like it's now the Reiner money—poor old fool," Vivian continued, as though she hadn't spoken. "By now he must know you're crazy."

Barbara threw up her hands in frustration. "We were supposed to be talking about your daughter and the things she got up to."

Vivian gave her a look of utter contempt. "You surely can't think you can turn me against my daughter? You can't think you can turn me against my beloved grandson? I don't give a damn who Chrissie's father is. My daughter Charlotte is his mother, and *I'm* his grandfather."

"Costello is his *father*!" Barbara shouted. "So that's your answer, is it? You don't mind that Rohan Costello is the boy's father? Rohan Costello—who let *our* boy drown?"

"Oh, Mum!" Charlotte moaned in despair, thanking God Christopher was far away in his room.

Vivian Marsdon was so angry he was temporarily unable to speak. "I should have stopped you, Barbara," he said grimly after a few moments. "I shouldn't have let you crucify young Costello and his mother—a struggling young woman you had once helped. Losing Mattie has deranged you. You desperately needed counselling at the time. I should have seen you got it. Instead I let you wreck your mental health and the Costellos' lives. Rohan was *not* to blame for Mattie's death. It was a tragic accident. I've long since accepted that."

"So he's not so bad. Is that it?" Barbara asked, breathing heavily. "You can adjust?"

"I may need a little time." Vivian turned to his daughter. "It's true, Charlie?"

"Of course it's true," Barbara cut in. "I don't go around making up stories."

"Keep out of this, Barbara," Vivian Marsdon warned. "I'm running out of patience with you."

Barbara gave a shriek of horror. "Patience? I just got here."

Charlotte ignored her mother. "Yes, Dad. But I believed when I married Martyn I was carrying his child."

"What else do you need, Vivian? A blasted DNA report?"

"Shut up, woman," Vivian Marsdon thundered, shocked

at his ex-wife's vindictiveness. "If you can't shut up then I'll show you the door." He had never sounded so authoritative.

Barbara Reiner reeled back in her chair. "I—beg—your—pardon?" She could scarcely believe her ears.

"Please…please stop. Both of you," Charlotte begged. "Marrying Martyn was a huge mistake, but I didn't know what else to do at the time. It wasn't as though you were here for me, Mum. I didn't have the guts to tell Dad I was pregnant. I didn't have the guts to go it alone."

"Go it alone?" Barbara repeated with scorn. "You took all the comfort you could from poor Martyn, though, didn't you? So much for your endless love for Costello!"

Charlotte met her mother's hard, accusatory gaze. "I *did* go to Martyn for comfort. I was missing Rohan terribly. We'd been friends all our lives."

"And you used him," Barbara condemned.

"I suppose I did." It had never for a second entered her head to abort her child. But she couldn't have turned to Rohan when she was carrying Martyn's child. There'd be no way out of it. She'd married Martyn.

"That's it. That's enough, Barbara," Vivian Marsdon said sternly. "How could Charlie go to you? Her mother? You were never the soul of comfort at the best of times. You spent all the years of Mattie's life dancing attendance on him."

"Because he was delicate, you ignorant fool!"

"The bitter truth was you spoonfed him. You would never listen to me—"

Charlotte cut in. "Please keep your voices down. I couldn't bear for Christopher to hear you."

"He won't hear us, Charlie." Vivian reached out to pat her hand. "His bedroom is too far away."

"Just as well." Charlotte shuddered. "What did you hope to achieve, Mum, by coming here?"

Barbara straightened her shoulders. "I need your word, Charlotte, that you won't marry Costello. I couldn't live with that. If you give me your promise there's no more to be said. You can carry on with your charade."

Charlotte stared back at her mother in wonderment. So wonderfully elegant on the outside, a total mess within. "I'm afraid there's no question of that. Rohan recognised his son the instant he laid eyes on him."

"Did he really?" Vivian Marsdon turned to his daughter, showing his shock.

"As per usual, Vivian, you've had your head in the sand," his ex-wife said contemptuously. "The boy will grow into the image of him. Those blue eyes, for a start. One rarely sees eyes like that. Are you *really* prepared to create a great scandal, Charlotte? For Costello? He's making quite a name for himself in the city. An illegitimate child won't help. Or the mother of his child marrying his childhood friend. What about the Valley? The news would shock the entire district. God alone knows what the Prescotts will think, let alone *do*."

"They'll do nothing," Vivian Marsdon said, his eyes on fire.

"They won't have to. There are few things Nicole and her mother like better than airing their suspicions," Charlotte said. "Rohan and I are prepared to wear it all. One can't hide the truth for ever."

"Just another nine-day wonder," Vivian Marsdon said with a hopeful smile. There would be a scandal. No question. But it was high time he came out on the side of his long-suffering daughter. "Good God, woman, Costello has bought Riverbend. He has big plans for it. Christopher is his son and heir. Christopher will one day inherit his birthright. Think of that. The wheel of fortune has turned full circle. Marsdons planted the first vines in the Valley, the first olive groves. We won't just be selling our harvested crops. I've heard Costello is planning to build a new winery. Bring in all the best people. I believe he's already having talks with the von Luckners—father and son. Remember old Konrad predicted young Rohan would have a splendid future?"

That was true. The von Luckners were members of a very posh clan from Germany, who had migrated shortly before the First World War to get away from Europe.

"Who told you, Dad?" It was no secret the von Luckners were in need of a big inflow of cash to expand and continue the late Erich von Luckner's bold vision.

"My dear girl, people tell me things. Always have. I am a Marsdon—a community leader."

"So, you're all going to finish up *friends*?" Barbara cried out in disbelief, appalled that things weren't going as she'd planned.

"There are worse things than friends, Barbara. Like ex-wives." Vivian glanced down pointedly at his watch. "Shouldn't you be getting back to poor old Reiner? I suppose he let you have the Bentley without a whimper?"

CHAPTER NINE

AFTER Barbara had left, acting as though she was cut to the quick by their refusal to heed her warnings, father and daughter returned to the living room, their hearts heavy.

"This is my fault," Charlotte said, her psyche so wounded by years of blame she sought not one ounce of sympathy for herself.

"Of course it isn't," groaned her father. "Was that *really* the woman I married?" he asked in genuine wonder. "What's bugging her most, do you suppose? The fact that you're going to marry Rohan Costello? That's he's Christopher's father? Or that you slept with poor old Martyn too? She always did take his side, you know. She believed Martyn's version of events over yours. Rohan never defended himself."

"He didn't have to, Dad. Rohan was an innocent victim. I was only with Martyn *once* before we were married." She turned her beautiful eyes on her father. There really had to be something wrong with her. Post-traumatic stress? That was a popular diagnosis. Terrible things happened, yet they were never mentioned. Abuses of all kinds. Perhaps she should get a big sheet of cardboard and write *Rape* on it? It wasn't going to trip off her tongue.

"What awful luck! It's women who pay the price, isn't

it? Women who get hurt the most. We weren't there for you, Charlie. And you were so young."

She couldn't bear to talk about it any more. Had she been able to depend upon a loving, wise mother, her life might have turned out differently.

Charlotte turned her head, as though her son might suddenly appear. "It's a wonder Chris hasn't come downstairs," she said, with a puzzled frown. "He would have seen the Bentley leave."

"We did tell him to remain in his room. He's a good boy, and a highly intuitive one. He knew there was going to be trouble. Barbara doesn't care how many casualties there are in her one-woman war."

"I'm so sorry, Dad."

"Oh, for God's sake, Charlie! It's your parents who should be sorry. You've had some very difficult episodes in your life. Mostly because we failed you—your mother and I. We failed the Costellos. We failed Martyn. He should have been made to retract his damaging statements. It's a wonder you have any love left for me."

Did one ever lose the capacity to love a parent? Even a bad one? "Plenty of love!" Charlotte rose to her feet, dropping a kiss on her father's silver-streaked blond head. "I'll look in on Chris, then make us both a strong cup of coffee."

"I'll get things going." Vivian stood up. On the surface he was calm enough; underneath he was full of intense regrets about his own past behaviour and horror at his ex-wife's lack of compassion. "Did you hear the way that woman spoke to us?" he huffed. "I'll tell you this: she won't put a foot inside the door again."

"Try to put it out of your mind, Dad," Charlotte advised.

"With Mattie gone, love is something Mum *cannot* provide. I think of her as not being in her *right* mind."

"One wonders if she ever was."

All was quiet inside when Charlotte knocked on her son's door. "It's me, Chris. You can come out now, darling. Sorry it took so long."

She waited for him to come to the door, full of questions. Gifted children had many advantages. They also suffered disadvantages. They recognised too much, too early. Maybe he was taking a nap? He hadn't been feeling one hundred per cent, but as usual he made no complaints.

"Chrissie?" She knocked again, and then when she got no response, opened the door.

The room was empty. She sucked in her breath. He had to be in the bathroom just down the hall. Maybe he'd been sick again? She hoped not. She had thought the short bout of vomiting the night before was over.

"Chrissie, love?" She knocked on the bathroom door. "Are you sick again?"

Again no response. She opened the door, taking in the empty white and turquoise tiled bathroom at a glance. Where was he? It was too early for her to be worried, yet she felt a chill run right through her body. Was it possible Christopher had crept down the stairs to listen in on the adult conversation? Would he do that? Had he heard his grandfather's lion-like roar? That would have put him on the alert. Christopher was a great one for knowing the facts. Why had his grandmother come visiting? They rarely saw her. Why had his grandfather shouted in that angry voice?

It was possible—more than possible—her son had decided to find out. Christopher was no ordinary child.

Oh, God! Oh, God! Was it happening all over again? A missing child? A mother's worst nightmare short of a child's confirmed death. Swiftly she got a hold on herself, trying to think things through. She had to accept now that he *had* listened in. Made the choice to run. Run where? Could he have gone to Peter's place? Could he have sought the comfort of his best friend? She hurried away to put a call through to Peter's house. Pray God he was there. Peter would be home from school by now.

Rohan's secretary, Shona, appeared at the door, her pretty face without its usual dimpled smile. "I know you told me to hold your calls, Rohan, but I think you'll want to take this one. It's Charlotte. She sounds very distressed."

"Right, put it through." He was scheduled to meet up with one of his more important clients, but if there was anything wrong with Charlotte he would cancel.

Under fifteen minutes later he was in the air, the company helicopter heading for Riverbend. Children were life itself to their parents. He had found Charlotte. He had found his son. Nothing would be allowed to put their future in jeopardy. He knew Charlotte's fears were gaining momentum with every passing hour, but what he had seen of his son gave him hope. A boy under tremendous stress, he had gone off on his own. Maybe he should have told his mother first. But he had needed to do some thinking alone. He had a strong feeling Christopher had inherited his temperament.

The instant she heard the *thrump-thrump* of the rotors Charlotte was flying out through the door, feeling as though if anyone could find Christopher it would be Rohan—his father. She hurled herself at him, the bone-deep stabs of fear abating to a level she could bear. It was torture to think her seven-year-old son had had to run away to counteract the shock and the grief he must have felt as powerful deceptions were exposed. Would she ever be the same for him again? Would his great love for her, his faith in her, change?

Rohan caught her up, pulling her close into his body. Her anguish couldn't have been more visible. "I spotted the police car and the scouters from the air," he said, his cheek against her thick curtain of hair. "There are a lot of people out there, all up and down the riverbank."

The river.

A half-forgotten poem sprang disturbingly into his head.

Whoever said happiness is the light shining on the water?
The water is cold and dark and deep.

There could *never* be another drowning. That was his belief, and it was strong. He wasn't about to panic. Mattie wouldn't allow it. Mattie who had ceased to be and yet lived on.

"Practically the whole village is out." Charlotte's willowy body was shaking like a leaf. "Where *is* he, Rohan?" She stared up into his brilliant eyes as though he alone knew the answer.

He took her firmly by the shoulders. "Wherever he is, Charlotte, he's *safe*. He loves you far too much to do anything silly. He's a clever, thoughtful child. He wants to be by himself right now. He wants to sort everything out in his own mind. I used to go off by myself, remember?"

"Yes, you did." She felt a flutter of hope.

"I can tell you one thing," Rohan said grimly. "Your

mother will never be allowed near Christopher again. Where's your father?"

He put his arm around her waist, leading her back into the house. She was trying so hard to be brave. That was the thing! Charlotte *was* brave. And she had never been one to tell even the smallest lie. It wasn't a matter of degree with Charlotte. A lie was a lie was a lie! Even now her inexplicable action in marrying Martyn brought him to near breaking point. Only he didn't have the time now for all the convolutions of his mind.

"Dad is out searching," Charlotte said. "He's tremendously upset. I shouldn't say this, but I'm feeling near hatred for my mother. She provoked this thing. Dad went off in a sick rage. He loves Christopher."

"I know. There are too many people searching the riverbanks. Christopher isn't there."

She lifted her eyes to him, tears welling. "But how can we be sure of that, Rohan? What Chrissie learned would have destroyed all his certainties about life. About me—his mother. About *you*—his real flesh-and-blood father. He's only a little boy, no matter how intelligent. What he overheard would have been shocking to his ears. Who knows what a child in shock will do?"

He bent to stay her quivering mouth with a kiss. "Mattie won't let Christopher fall in the river."

Her expression totally changed. "You're saying that as though Mattie is still alive and breathing."

"So what if he isn't? He's still out there. Somewhere. Parallel universe—who knows? I continue to feel a spiritual connection to my childhood friend. I don't go around analysing it. It just *is*. Christopher wouldn't do anything so radical, anyway. He knows Mattie's story. He's a child with deep feelings. He's trying to understand what he heard. Weigh it up. I'll get the Sergeant to direct more searchers to the vineyards and the olive groves. But somehow I don't think he's there. The old winery?"

"It's been searched. The house has been searched from top to bottom." She meant the Riverbend mansion.

"Right—well, I'm off!" He spoke with immense purpose.

"I'm coming with you." A tear ran down her cheek. She dashed it away. She would search until she dropped down dead.

Only Rohan wasn't having it. "I know how hard this is for you, Charlie, but you must stay here," he said with quiet authority. "For all we know Christopher could work his way back. We don't want him returning to an empty house."

"But, Rohan—he must have heard all the commotion." She was ready to argue, her nerves strung taut. This was her son. *Their* son. "The noise of the chopper arriving. I'm so frightened. I've spent so many years of my life frightened."

No time either for him to question *that* shock admission. *Years of her life frightened?* He knew next to nothing about her life with Martyn. She wouldn't tell him. "Well, I'm here now." He let her body slump against him, feed off his strength. "And I won't be back until I find our son. Trust me, Charlotte."

"With my life!" She looked up at him, her heart in her eyes. "With our son's life. Forgive me, Rohan. I've made so many mistakes. And now our son knows them." A sound of agony escaped her lips. "He thought me perfect. He won't any more. Rohan, he mightn't even *love* me any more. The thought is too dreadful!"

He took her beautiful, agonised face between his hands. "Christopher can no more stop loving you than I can." He spoke not gently, but with some force. Enough force to close out certain fears from her mind. "What you have to do is remember you're at the very *centre* of our lives. Hold the thought close. I'll find him." He bent his head and kissed her hard.

It had been dark for well over an hour. Wherever Christopher was, he surely must have heard their raised voices. The whole area was ringing with the echoes of his name. People, truly chilled by the turn of events, were loath to return home. Even Gordon Prescott, deeply distressed, had called in to the Lodge to express his concerns, then set out with Charlotte's father, friends from childhood. The searchers would come out again at first light, but the darkness was complete.

Were the Marsdons jinxed? For that matter the Prescotts? Both families, so closely entwined, had suffered tragedies, and that was the question people were asking themselves. The atmosphere all along the riverbank had struck many a soul as extremely spooky. They all knew Matthew Marsdon's tragic story. They had been given instructions where to search. Every last man and woman hoped they would be the one to find the boy safe. But the more time that elapsed, the more fearful the searchers became. A seven-year-old child in peril! It struck at the heart of every parent.

Why had the boy taken off? All they had been told was that he had most probably overheard a family argument and become upset. Quite a few people had seen the big Bentley driving through the area, the ex-Mrs Marsdon sitting regally in its back seat, a uniformed chauffeur up front. Once a very highly regarded woman, Barbara Reiner as she was now had taken a nosedive in the popularity stakes. The love and attention she had lavished on her son had left her only daughter out in the cold. Small wonder

Charlotte Prescott's marriage hadn't worked. The feeling at the time had been that it was a marriage of convenience. And some reckoned she'd just *had* to be pregnant when she walked reed-slim down the aisle. What did it matter anyway? Charlotte Prescott was a beautiful young woman. Inside and out. Her son had to be found.

Alive.

Rohan didn't know the moment the answer to the question of Christopher's whereabouts came to him. Was it Christopher's guardian angel whispering in his ear? Or Mattie? Or maybe Mattie had been elected for the job?

He commandeered one of the search vehicles, a utility truck, and sped off. It didn't make a lot of sense, but that didn't matter. He had the strong conviction Christopher had headed off to the cottage where Rohan and his mother had lived. He thought now he had made some comment about it to Christopher—about the place where he and his mother had lived for the first seventeen years of his life.

As if a button had been pushed, there was a shift in his thinking. He remembered how he had pointed out his grandmother's old cottage to Christopher from the helicopter. The cottage had long been empty. He knew the land—not valuable—had been bought for future development, but so far nothing had happened. The timber structure appeared to be settling down into the earth. The white picket fence had a great many broken teeth. The corrugated iron roof, once a bright red, was thickly sown with dead foliage from the overhanging canopy of trees. What had been the small front and back gardens were overrun by long grass and vegetation gone wild. It was a veritable jungle now. The old cottage where he had grown up on the wrong side of the tracks was an abandoned old derelict.

There was no moon tonight. It was as black as only

country black could be. No street lights to pierce the darkness. He had a heavy-duty torch with him on the passenger seat. Would his boy be shrinking from the darkness? Would he be sitting frozen with fear of snakes? Would he be desperately regretting what he had done?

Rohan drove the utility truck right through what had been the front gate, jamming on the brakes at the base of the short flight of steps. He swung out of the vehicle, leaving the headlights on.

"Christopher!" he shouted, running up onto the verandah, hoping the old boards would take his weight. "It's me. It's Rohan. You must come out. You're a responsible boy. Your mother is sick with worry. So is your grandfather. People have been searching for you for hours. Come out now. You're quite safe. I'm here now. I'll never leave you again. That's my solemn promise, Christopher. Come out, son. We need to get you home."

The front door lay open, hanging on its hinges. Vandals? Or simply years of no one caring what happened to the place. Having accomplished so much, Rohan was having difficulty accepting he and his mother had ever lived in such a place—but then his mother had kept the cottage spotlessly clean. He had helped her put in a vegetable garden at the back. He had cut the grass while his mother had looked after the beds of perennials around the picket fence.

He moved into the house, shining the torch down the hallway that ran from front to back. God! He could cover it in less than half a dozen paces.

"I know you're here, Christopher," he called, gentling the urgency of his voice. "I know you're frightened. But there's nothing to be frightened about. I used to run off myself when I was a boy and things got too much for me to handle. I know how you feel. But your mother and I want you to come home. Please, Christopher. There are always things in life we have to face. We have to swallow our fears. Find our courage. Come out now. Let me see you. We can confront what is worrying you together."

Rohan didn't even consider he was talking to an empty old house. Christopher, his son, was here somewhere.

A moment later a small boy stumbled out of what had been the kitchen and into the hallway, vigorously rubbing his eyes. "I'm a real sook," he announced, in a quavery voice he tried hard to make stronger. "I've been crying."

Rohan thought he would never forget this moment. Huge relief bubbled up in his chest. He moved towards his son, feeling such a rush of love he couldn't begin to describe it. "Grown men cry, Christopher," he said, unbearably touched by the way this small boy was trying to hold himself together. "There's no shame in shedding a few tears. Come here to me."

"I wanted to see where you'd lived," Christopher explained, starting towards the wonderful man he had been drawn to on sight. "Are you my *real* dad?" he asked, realising with a pang of sadness that he had been having difficulty remembering the man he had once called Daddy for some time.

Rohan reached for his son, fragile as a bird in his strong grip. He lifted him high in his arms. "I *am* your father, Christopher," he said. "I am so very, *very* sorry for the confusion that's gone on." That surely couldn't be the best way to put it to a child? Rohan agonised. *Confusion?* He could hardly say he hadn't even known he existed until very recently. "I *want* to be your father. I want to do everything I can for you and your mother. How does that feel?"

Christopher had already reached his decision. He buried his hot, sweaty little face in his father's neck. "Real *good*!" he said.

* * *

Rohan used his mobile to have the search called off. News that young Christopher Prescott had been found safe and sound flew around the network. And Rohan, in a matter of days, was to make a sizeable and very welcome contribution to the Valley's Search and Rescue Team.

All's well that ends well—was the general view. One had to keep a close eye on kids. They created problems without meaning to. Sometimes awful things happened in communities. This, by the grace of God, wasn't one of them. Lots of people believed in guardian angels. Young Christopher Prescott obviously had one. And Rohan Costello, absent so long from Silver Valley, had managed to channel that guiding light.

They were safe. Both of them were safe. Christopher and Rohan. The joy of it swamped her. The exterior lights lit up the garden, and the Jeep had barely come to a stop when Christopher opened the door and jumped out onto the gravel.

"Mummy!" he cried, as though the sight of her had put his world right.

The love in her son's voice, the expression on his dirty, tear-streaked face, told Charlotte that whatever she had done her seven-year-old son was one person who wasn't going to hold her to blame.

"Chrissie!" She caught him to her, hugged and patted him hard, folded him into a mutual display of love. "Thank God you're safe."

Christopher pulled back a little, tilting his head. "It was Rohan who found me." He slanted his rescuer, who stood leaning against the Jeep, a beaming glance.

"Of course it was." Charlotte breathed in air. Breathed, *breathed*. Of course she'd known her little son would come back to her. Hadn't she?

She turned her head, binding Rohan to her with a glance. He had made the decision to remain on the periphery, clearly giving them a minute together. Her father, who had been positioned behind her at the front door, anxiously awaiting their arrival, had joined in the reunion, his long arms now making a cocoon around his daughter and his grandson.

"Christopher, you must never run off and scare us again," he scolded, making a sudden change of direction now the boy was safe. "We're endlessly grateful to you, Rohan," he called to the tall, handsome, self-contained young man standing apart. "It's a miracle you thought of the old cottage. Christopher could have been out all night. Come in, come in," he invited, with the warmth of a man who had decided to put the traumas of the past behind them. "Let me get you a well-deserved drink."

"It was so dark I couldn't see a thing," Christopher announced. "Rohan said I have to apologise to everyone who came out to search for me. Of course I will. But I never thought people would be going to look for me. Only you and Grandpa, Mummy. Rohan wasn't coming back until the weekend. He told me before he went away."

"God only knows—" Vivian Marsdon started in exasperation, then stopped. "There was a good chance your mother wouldn't have been able to contact Rohan, Christopher," he said after a moment.

"Let's drop it for now." Charlotte tapped her father's shoulder. "Chris needs a nice long shower, and when he's done he can have something to eat. Then bed."

"My stomach is groaning. I feel really hungry. There was no water at the cottage either. I'm sorry everyone was worried, but I wanted to go somewhere I could think."

His grandfather frowned. "You might have had to spend the night there, my boy."

"I think I fell asleep, but I can't be sure."

"Well, no harm's done." Rohan intervened smoothly. "I'll have that drink, Mr Marsdon, if it's okay?" He moved into the pool of light.

"Please, please—it's Vivian," Vivian Marsdon insisted, waving a welcoming hand. "I'll join you."

Charlotte and Rohan exchanged wry glances at her father's dramatic turnaround. "I'll take Chrissie off," she said. "Could you make him a sandwich, Dad? He can have a glass of milk with it."

"Put some Milo in it, please, Grandpa?" Christopher requested.

He turned his blond head to address his saviour, who just happened to be his father. He didn't know how it had happened, but he was sure his mother would explain it properly to him. He had a feeling Rohan wanted to hear too. Was it *confusion* that had put his grandmother into such a terrible spin? He hadn't waited on the stairs to hear all she had to say. The awful grating sound in her voice had made him feel sick. He had just wanted to get away from the house.

"You're going to wait for me, aren't you, Rohan?" He held his small body very still, awaiting his hero's answer.

"Yes, I am, chief!" Rohan gave his son a reassuring smile.

Christopher beamed. "Oh, good! Rohan and I are mates, Mummy. I'm his mate. He's my mate." He turned to Rohan, giving him a confidential man-to-man look. "I'll keep calling you Rohan for a while—just like you said, Rohan."

"Good thinking!" Rohan touched his fingertips to his forehead in a tiny salute.

Christopher burst out laughing, then sobered abruptly. He shot his mother an apprehensive look. "Grandmother's gone, hasn't she?"

"Too right she has!" his grandfather answered, his deep

voice rising, the vein in the middle of his forehead twitch-
ing away. "And she won't be coming back in a hurry."

"Does she know I ran away?" Christopher asked as his
mother led him off.

"She will when she checks her e-mails." Vivian Marsdon
smiled grimly. "Go along now, Christopher. You've worn
us all out."

Charlotte and Rohan walked into Riverbend's entrance
hall hand in hand, although both were aware of the intense
strain between them. Christopher had been found. The
danger was over. But she knew there were many questions that were going to be asked. The problem was she
didn't know how she was going to answer Rohan, let alone
find acceptable answers for their son. Highly intelligent
Christopher might be, but he was still only a boy of seven.
Plenty of time for him to find out how babies were made.

He had fallen asleep almost as soon as his head hit the
pillow. Her father, who had put in some deeply harrowing
hours searching for his grandson, had joined Christopher
with his sandwiches, substituting a nice drop of Laphroaig
for milk and a couple of teaspoons of Milo. Rohan had
accepted a single malt whisky, but declined a chicken
sandwich. He had contacted his housekeeper at the house,
he explained. Dinner would be waiting. He had turned
his dark head to invite Charlotte to join him—a naturally
commanding young man, who wasn't going to accept a
refusal.

She'd had absolutely no idea what response her father
would make. He was a man of the old school who regarded
himself as the head of family, to be deferred to no matter
what one's age or status in life. Would he say it might be
best if she remained at home? As it was, she had every
intention of returning to the Lodge late. Christopher might

very well awaken during the night. He had, after all, suffered his own trauma.

Instead Vivian Marsdon now walked them to the front door, where he paused to look at the younger man, his expression that of a man who had set aside time to put a nagging concern in order. "I want to tell you, Rohan, I deeply regret what has gone before." He fetched up a great sigh. "I can't, of course, change anything. None of us can. But I allowed my wife to control the whole terrible situation surrounding Mattie's death. Like a fool, I couldn't see what was under my nose. I'd very much appreciate it now, Rohan, if we could be friends?" He held out his hand, the tone of his deep, rich voice absolutely sincere.

This was the moment when Rohan would be well within his rights to reject an overture that had come far too late. Instead, without a moment's hesitation, he took Vivian Marsdon's hand in a brief, firm grip. "I'd like that, sir."

"Good. Good." Vivian coloured, fiercely pleased. He bent down to kiss his daughter's cheek. "Go along now, Charlie. Enjoy dinner. Relax your nerves. I'm sure you two have lots to talk about. I'll leave the light on for you."

"Thanks, Dad." Charlotte gave her father a lovely tender smile. "Chris was pretty much exhausted, but I'd like to check on him during the night."

"Hungry?" Rohan led the way past the grand reception rooms to the state-of-the-art kitchen.

"Not really, thank you, Rohan." Hours of the most intense anxiety had shocked hunger out of her.

He studied her intently, noting the haunted expression in her green eyes, the way she held her slender body taut. "Better have something all the same." He was reminded of the way she had looked on that long-ago terrible day at the river. Both of them had suffered more than their fair share of grief.

"I shouldn't stop too long." Her eyes were stinging. What must he think of her? Rohan had always been her greatest friend. He had made her happier than anyone else in the world. He had been her truly glorious lover, was the father of her child. But she couldn't rid herself of the thought that she had lost his trust for ever. That weighed very heavily on her.

Louise Burch, the housekeeper, came bustling through the swinging kitchen door, leaving tantalising aromas in her wake. "Good evening, sir. Good evening, Mrs Prescott. I should have met you at the door," she apologised, sounding a little short of breath. "I was just coming to check."

"Don't worry about that, Louise. Roy not home yet?" Roy Burch had been one of the searchers.

Louise's face lit up with a smile as she turned to Charlotte. "All of us are so happy and relieved young Christopher has been found, Mrs Prescott. Boys are such scamps. Roy went off with some of our friends to have a celebratory drink. I was going to join them."

"Then you mustn't wait," Rohan said immediately. "Charlotte and I can manage."

Louise Burch adopted her professional manner. "Thank you so much. There's roast chicken just out of the oven. Pesto and mascarpone sauce. Little chat potatoes, beans, and baby peas from the garden. I'll wait and serve up."

"No need for that, Mrs Burch," Charlotte intervened with a smile. "You go off now. My father and I are enormously grateful to all the good caring people in the Valley. I will be telling your husband that when I see him. There's no need for you to look after the two of us."

"Well, if you say so." Louse Burch glanced from one to the other. What beautiful young people they were!

"We *do* say so, Louise." Rohan gave her an easy smile.

Louise blushed. Talk about sex appeal! "Then thank you so much. That's very good of you."

"Not at all. And we'll clear away afterwards, so you're not to worry," Charlotte said.

Moments later, apron folded away, Mrs Burch took her leave. "By the way, I made a plum cake with plum syrup," she told them with a bright smile. "One of my specialities. Plenty of ice cream and whipped cream in the fridge."

"Thank you, Louise," said Rohan. "I'll probably have a very large slice."

Louise Burch went off beaming. She and her husband were more contented than they had ever been, looking after Mr Costello. He was the best boss in the world, and their bungalow in the grounds couldn't be more comfortable. Silver Valley was absolute heaven after their last job, with a demanding old matriarch. They had made friends in no time.

Charlotte Prescott, a widow, was so beautiful—and so young to have a seven-year-old child to rear alone. Wouldn't it be wonderful if she and Mr Costello made a match of it? A grand house like Riverbend needed a lady like that. Apparently Mrs Prescott's father had fallen on hard times and had had to sell the estate. If those two beautiful young people got married Charlotte Prescott would never have to leave her old home...

"Let's eat in here," Rohan said.

"Rohan?"

"No talk. I need to feed you first. Sit down before you fall down. I can get this."

He pulled out a chair for her at the long granite-topped table before moving away, super-efficient in everything he did. She watched him walk over to some impressive-looking refrigerated wine-storage cabinets, the contents on full view through the glass doors. He pulled out a bottle of white wine, showing her the label.

"Fine. Fine…" She glanced at it, looked away. It was an award-winning Chardonnay. She was trying hard not to let the tension inside her break the surface. "Not much dinner for me, Rohan." Under his smooth control, he too had to be fighting powerful feelings.

"When did you last eat?" He found glasses, then poured the perfectly chilled wine, passing a glass to her.

"When did *you*?" she countered.

"Around seven this morning. I don't often get a chance to stop for lunch, so at the moment I'm hungry. Charlotte, you didn't answer *my* question."

She stared up at him with troubled eyes. "I can't seem to find the right answers to your questions."

"That's because you're hiding so much."

She was wearing a soft georgette top of pastel colours, with an ankle-length matching skirt. The top had a low oval neckline that allowed just a glimpse of cleavage. The fabric clung to her small high breasts and showed off her taut torso and tiny waist. She looked like a top model—especially with her long blonde mane loose. He didn't think he could ever let her cut her hair. It was too beautiful.

"You don't trust me," she said sadly.

"I *half* trust you." He softened it with a smile.

"Well, that's better than nothing. But lack of trust ruins relationships, Rohan. Anyway, I made afternoon tea for my mother. I don't remember eating anything, but I did have a cup of tea."

"We won't talk about your mother." He was busy cutting

slices of tender white chicken breast. "Not for the moment anyway."

She had to be content with that.

As it turned out, he didn't appear to have an appetite either—though they had no difficulty finishing the bottle of wine. Both ate little of what otherwise would have been a delicious meal.

"Well, we can't disappoint Mrs Burch," Rohan said later, eyeing the plum cake. The table was cleared, dishes rinsed and stacked in the dishwasher. "You'll have to join me in a slice. It looks good."

"She's a good cook. Very good."

"I wouldn't have hired her otherwise. She's rather passionate about food. I like that." He cut a large slice and then, before Charlotte could voice any protest, cut it in two, giving Charlotte the narrow end, and pouring a little plum syrup over both sections. "All right. *Eat* that."

"You're ordering me about?"

"Yes," he said crisply, then sat down again.

She took hold of her cake fork. "You want to talk to me, don't you?"

"Charlotte, my love, I've *tried* talking to you." The expression in his eyes was hard; a mocking smile curled his mouth.

"You must think I'm pathetic."

He laughed without humour. "Would you like some cream?" He stood up.

"No, thank you."

"Well, I'll have some. I need sweetening up." He went to the large stainless steel refrigerator standing side by side with a matching freezer. "Second thoughts—ice cream. Seriously—won't you join me?"

"You're enjoying this in a weird sort of way, aren't you?"

"The hell I am! We've both had a shock. I'm trying my level best to be kind." He pointed to her plate.

"Okay, okay." She handed it up to him. It might even make her feel better.

He laid a nicely turned dessertspoonful of vanilla ice cream on it.

Charlotte made herself eat. Actually, it was lovely.

When they were finished he took the plates and cutlery from her, rinsed them, then put them in the dishwasher, turning it on. Finally he disposed of the empty wine bottle.

"You're very useful in the kitchen." She gave in to a wry little laugh.

"Just one of my many talents. I'm pretty useful in the bedroom as well. And you don't hold back there, do you, Charlotte? Believe me, you're the best of the best. The cool, cool, touch-me-not is an enormous turn-on. Charlotte hiding her passionate nature."

The passionate nature only you unlocked, she thought. What a tremendous burden would be lifted from her if she could give voice to her heart!

You must help me, Rohan. I'm a damaged woman.

Seriously messed-up, too young, and with no one to turn to, to ease her out of it. It happened so much in life. She'd thought she didn't have a choice. She'd taken the wrong direction. She had married the wrong man.

"Would you like coffee?"

Rohan was desperate to make some breakthrough.

He loved this woman. Nothing could change that. Not even the fact she had rejected him for Martyn Prescott, who'd been able to give her every material thing in life. Her decision had troubled her deeply. Unfortunately one always paid in the end for bad decisions. He still wanted Charlotte very badly, and wondered whatever had happened to something called pride. Maybe love and pride didn't go together? He had been committed to Charlotte Marsdon from childhood. They were the legendary childhood sweethearts.

She stood up, her graceful body set in determined lines. "I should go."

"In a little while. You might consider *I* won't be able to rest until I hear what your mother had to say. What my son overheard."

"He didn't tell you?" She bent her shining head, almost as if in prayer.

"I didn't like to question him. It was enough to have him safe. If you must know, I think Christopher is as confused as I am. That was the fool word I had to use with him. *Confusion.* Isn't that a sick joke? There was *confusion* over who exactly was his father. Well, at least he knows now—and he seems pretty happy about it. So thank God for that! Let's go back into the living room. You're going to have to open up a little, Charlotte. If only for our son's sake."

He came around to her, taking her firmly by her upper arms.

For a split second she was elsewhere. A different time. A different place. A very different man. Bad memories surfaced, caught her up so strongly she visibly cringed. Then, realising what she had done—this was *Rohan*—she took a great gulp of air.

Rohan stared at her, astounded. "I can't possibly be hurting you." Nevertheless he slackened his grip. "For God's sake, Charlotte, what's *that* all about?"

She put her hand to her mouth. She was a mere heartbeat

away from telling him the whole shocking story. Only then she would lose his respect.

"You just *cringed* from me." Rohan tried very hard to speak gently. "Surely you didn't think I was about to hit you?"

"Of course not." She cursed herself for her involuntary action. "To tell the truth, I don't know what I'm doing."

"Charlotte, I wouldn't *dream* of hurting you."

"Rohan, I know that." She gave a desperate little moan, spent with emotion, letting her head fall forward against his chest.

"What am I going to do with you?" He began to rock her light body as if she were an inconsolable child. He'd used to think it quite possible to die of love for Charlotte. He still did. "You can't put me off, Charlotte." He lifted her chin, seeing his reflection in her eyes. "Tell me exactly what Christopher heard. Only then will I take you home. It's up to you. I need to be able to combat the fears my son has. We can't keep our history under wraps for much longer. Your father might have had blinkers on, but anyone with a sharp pair of eyes in their head will recognise me in Christopher. We both know that. It's all going to come out."

"I know." There was absolute certainty in her voice.

"You say that like you're in despair." He was grappling with the sexual hunger that had started to roar through him. "Don't you *want* the world to know Christopher is my son?"

She pressed her fingers against his mouth. "Rohan, the news will shock so many people. I don't really count my ex-in-laws among them—" she laughed raggedly "—but I must tell you I'm *elated* Chrissie has taken the revelation you're his real father in his stride. It has to be some deep primal recognition. But he must be wondering how it all happened. How I married Martyn. How we are Prescotts. And there's Martyn's tragic accident. Sooner or later someone is going to tell him there was a young woman in the car with the man he thought was his father. God, *I* can't handle it all. How can *he*? He's seven years old."

"Well, he's doing fine so far," Rohan pointed out tersely. "Come into the living room. We can work it out together, Charlotte. Life is full of revelations. People have to live with them every day. Betrayed people. I want to marry you. I'm going to marry you. Christopher should never be parted from his mother, and he's my son. We can't go our separate ways. That's not possible. I want to look after you both. Maybe it isn't happening the way I always planned, but it *is* happening. And soon."

He didn't say a word until she had finished telling him of her mother's visit. "She couldn't have been more unpleasant—"

"Vicious, don't you mean?" His fire-blue eyes blazed.

"She didn't know Christopher was at home." Of all things, she was now defending her indefensible mother. "The *one* day he misses school, my mother turns up."

"Christopher said he ran off before he heard the lot."

"He heard more than enough," she said painfully. "He heard my mother say I had sex with you *and* Martyn."

"Well, you did, didn't you?" he challenged bleakly. "Does he know what 'having sex' means?"

She was so upset she averted her face. "The things he knows *amaze* me. I don't know if he's got right down to the *'hows'*. Dad is very involved in his education. They do a lot together. But Dad would never get into that particular area. He would regard Chrissie as far too young. It's all history, geography, the moon, the stars, the earth—things like that."

"Oh, Charlotte!" He felt close to defeat. "What happened to us?"

A great swath of her hair fell forward against her cheek. "I'm not proud of myself, Rohan. But I have to ask you to take pity on me. I can't take any more tonight. Tomorrow, maybe."

"Okay. I'll take you home. I have to go back to Sydney in the morning. I have an important meeting I had to cancel today. You'll be all right? I'll come back as soon as I can. We have to decide what's best to do. Your father has had a big shock too."

Charlotte gave a little sob. "There's no accounting for reactions. He did get a shock, but he's over it already. My mother's *performance* guaranteed that. You know, he's wasted years pining for her."

His mouth twisted at the irony. "Well, now he's seen her true colours. Your father is a handsome, virile man. He should remarry."

"Maybe he might now. Lord knows there are several very attractive eligible women in the Valley who would jump at the chance of becoming the second Mrs Marsdon. The years that one wastes!" She lifted her eyes to his. They were full of tears.

"Charlie, don't do this," he groaned, his voice deepening with emotion. "I hunger and thirst for you. I want to keep you here, but I can't. Don't cry. *Please*. You cry, and I warn you my feelings will get the better of me."

"So take me home," she burst out wildly, and yet she surged towards him.

He caught her as she all but threw herself at him, trying to suppress the raging fire of desire before it got totally out of hand.

"Rohan, I'm so *afraid*!"

"Of what? *Tell* me." He felt overwhelmingly protective.

"Of the things that might happen."

"So we've got a fair bit of explaining to do?" He thought that was what she meant. Gently he smoothed damp strands of her hair from her face. "We'll do it together. We speak to the Prescotts together. You clearly think they've had suspicions for some time. Did you love Martyn? Just a little? It's okay to tell me."

Once she'd had a good deal of affection for Martyn. As had he. Martyn Prescott had been an integral part of their daily lives.

"Who said anything about my loving Martyn?"

She'd shocked him with her throbbing answer. The *sob* in her voice. The sheer force of *repugnance* in her face. The stormy expression that swept into her lustrous green eyes took him totally unawares.

He stared down at her. "You blamed him for all the women? Martyn wasn't *really* a womaniser. He was obsessed with *you*. Perhaps he went after comfort elsewhere when you couldn't give him what he wanted?'

"Don't think I didn't try!" Her response was fiery. "I married him. I told you—I thought my unborn child was his. I thought I had a duty to marry him. You were thousands of miles away, on the other side of the continent. Four months can be an eternity. You thought money was important to me. It wasn't. *You* were. You have the mindset of a man who thinks his main job in life is to offer the woman he loves security."

"Well, isn't it?" He caught her beautiful face in his two hands, her hair a golden cloud around her face.

"No—no!"

He'd had enough. More than enough. Heart hammering,

he stopped her mouth with his own, taking a firm and desperate hold on her as though he would never let her get away. Only she returned his deep, passionate kiss, pressing her body ever closer against his, her own hunger, longing, love, hot and fierce.

"Charlotte!" At the fervour of her response, his hand moved to her breast. He knew the flimsy top would come off easily. Next the skirt. He belonged to this woman and no one else. She belonged to him.

Both of them had caught fire. Their mouths remained locked until they had to draw apart just to catch breath. There was no question of stopping. No question of saying *no* to the ecstasy on offer. They only had to come together for the fires of desire to crackle, burn, and then within moments turn into a raging inferno.

He drew her down onto the rug where they stood.

CHAPTER TEN

CHRISTOPHER, surprisingly none the worse for the traumatic events of the day before, insisted on going to school.

"I have to tell everyone I must have been delirious to do anything so stupid." He had worked out his explanation in advance. "I *did* have a high temperature, didn't I. Mummy?"

"Well, it didn't get to the scalding stage, but, yes, your temperature *was* higher than normal for some hours."

"Then that will have to do." He could never tell anyone the things his dreadful grandmother had screeched. He was still trying to figure them out.

"I'll come into school with you," Charlotte said. "Your headmaster turned out to search for you. So did the other teachers. I won't ever forget that."

Christopher looked more mortified than gratified. "I never knew people were going to search for me," he said unhappily. "I'll never do anything so stupid again."

She had to see the very calmness of his reaction had a great deal to do with his extraordinary emotional bond with Rohan. Rohan had come for him. Rohan had found him when no one else could. Rohan was now established as his *real* father, and that greatly reinforced Christopher's support base. Whatever the shock waves, they clearly hadn't overwhelmed their son. Christopher, a male child, saw

Rohan as supremely strong and capable. A father he could look up to. Two parents clearly *were* better than one. She agreed with that at every level.

The big dilemma actually centred around *her*. She had to go to her ex-in-laws and tell them exactly how it had been. She would not expose Martyn. She had no wish to bring extra pain on the Prescotts who, apart from Gordon, had never really treated her as "family". Every one in the Valley knew of the intense bond between her and the young Rohan Costello. Martyn came in second best. It didn't sit well with Mrs Prescott or Nicole, who had grown up unwavering in her jealousy of the young woman who became her sister-in-law. Charlotte always had the feeling Nicole would have been hostile towards her even if there had been no Rohan. Perhaps she had made Nicole feel wanting in the femininity stakes.

Mrs Ellory, the Prescotts' long-time housekeeper, greeted her at the door, remarkably pleased at seeing Charlotte again. She had been told when Charlotte was due to arrive, as Charlotte had rung ahead to ask if it would be convenient if she called in.

The answer from Mrs Prescott couldn't have been more direct. "Yes," she'd said, and hung up.

"And Christopher? He's all right this morning?"

Charlotte smiled, remembering how kind Mrs Ellory had been to her little boy. "Insisted on going to school."

"Amazing what children get up to," Mrs Ellroy said. "But all's well that ends well. Mrs Prescott and Nicole are waiting for you in the Garden Room, Charlotte. Go through. I'll be bringing morning tea directly. Lovely to see you, Charlotte. I've missed you and young Christopher."

"We've missed you too, Mrs Ellory." It was perfectly

true. Sometimes she had thought "Ellie", as Christopher had called her, was her only real friend in the house.

When Charlotte walked into the Garden Room, with its beautiful display of plants and hanging baskets, neither her ex-mother-in-law nor Nicole spoke.

So that was the way it was going to be.

It was extremely unnerving, but she had to steel her resolve. If she and Rohan were to marry in a few months' time there were facts all of them had to contend with. No matter how badly she wanted to be away from here, she had no option but to pay the Prescotts the courtesy of letting them know of her plans. Though nothing had been said, Charlotte felt in her bones Mrs Prescott had come to realise Christopher wasn't her grandson. But at the beginning Martyn had been so obsessive about her. It had been as though she was the only girl in the world who could make him happy. And what Martyn wanted, Martyn got.

Rohan concluded his meeting much earlier than expected. A successful deal had been struck, with big gains for both sides. There were other pressing matters that needed his attention, but he was feeling uncommonly anxious. He knew he and Charlotte had to confront the Prescotts. They had a need and a *right* to know what he and Charlotte had planned. Charlotte believed the Prescotts already knew Christopher wasn't Martyn's child, but it would have to be stated at their meeting. Secrets might take years to come out, but they rarely remained secret for ever. In their case, with Christopher so closely resembling Rohan, discovery was imminent.

He picked up the phone, requesting that the company helicopter—on stand-by—be ready for a return flight to the Valley. He needed to be with Charlotte. He felt deep inside him that life with Martyn had damaged her. That

MARGARET WAY   175

the once highly eligible and attractive Martyn Prescott, admired by many young women in the Valley, while full of fun and good company, had apparently not matured into a strong character. He had never apologised to him or his mother for the damaging scenario he had come up with for that tragic day on the river. That was the problem with Martyn. He couldn't accept responsibility for his actions. Martyn had made life far harder for Rohan and his innocent mother. He had turned Charlotte's mother against them. The outright lies and the half truths had left unresolvable griefs.

The Prescott housekeeper, Mrs Ellory, was passing through the entrance hall of High Grove as Rohan approached the front door. Vivian Marsdon had directed him there.

"Charlotte wanted to assure them Chrissie is safe. Also to thank Gordon, if he's around, for his efforts," Marsdon had said.

That piece of news had hit Rohan like an actual blow. "You shouldn't have let her go, sir. I told Charlotte when she decided it was time to talk to the Prescotts I would go with her. How long ago did she leave?"

"Not five minutes." Vivian had been thoroughly flustered. "That's why I'm so very surprised to see *you*. We thought you were staying in Sydney."

"I had concerns. Intuitions. Anyway, I can't stop. I'm going after her. Could I borrow your car?"

"Of course. I'll get the keys."

"Well, this *is* a day for nice surprises." Mrs Ellory came to the door to greet him. "You look marvellous, Rohan. I couldn't be more thrilled you're back in the Valley. People are quite excited by your plans. More jobs. More prosperity."

"I'm glad to hear that, Mrs Ellory," Rohan said, and, getting to the point, "Do you know where Charlotte is?"

"They're in the Garden Room—at the back of the house." She looked into Rohan Costello's blazing eyes. The boy Christopher had eyes like that. "I probably shouldn't say this, but I'm glad you're here. Charlotte needs support in this house. Do you want me to take you through?"

"I'll go the back way, Mrs Ellory. It's shorter."

"And you'll be able to gauge how things are going," she whispered back. "I only stay for Mr Prescott, you know. Mrs Prescott has turned into a very bitter woman. As for Nicole…!" She rolled her eyes.

Rohan gave her quick salute, then ran down a short flight of stone steps. He could hear raised voices as he rounded the side of the house.

Nicole. Such a difficult creature, Nicole. Martyn had inherited all the looks and the charm in the family.

"You're the very *opposite* of the way you look and sound!" the jealous and insecure young woman was lashing out.

"Oh, Nicole, do be quiet," her mother cut in sharply, as if to a child. "You brought nothing but suffering to my son, Charlotte. You couldn't face the world pregnant and unmarried, and Costello was nowhere around. But Martyn *was.* Martyn adored you. God knows why, when you were so involved with Costello. And Costello was dirt-poor. He had nothing. His mother struggled just to put food on the table. I paid her more than she was worth."

"Are you *serious*?" Charlotte countered, in a clear, firm voice.

Rohan knew perfectly well the right thing to do was to go in and announce himself. Instead he stood frozen, able to hear perfectly but unable to be seen. Maybe in staying where he was he could make some sense of everything that had transpired. Charlotte was keeping so much from him. It might advantage him to stay where he was until it became obvious she needed his help.

"You never overpaid *anyone*, Lesley. A plain statement of fact. You were tight-fisted with everyone but Martyn. Nicole missed out. You owed her far more time and attention. Gordon was the kind, generous one—"

"None of your business any more," Lesley Prescott cut her off, affronted. "So, you and Costello intend to marry?"

"That's what I've come to tell you, Lesley. You have a right to know."

"Oh, how simply wonderful that you think so!" Lesley Prescott crowed. "May I ask when the great day is to be?"

"Early next year."

"No doubt with your son as pageboy?" she sneered. "You take comfort where you can find it, don't you, Charlotte? Costello has made quite a name for himself now."

"You know he's Christopher's father?"

There was a terrible note in Lesley Prescott's voice. "We didn't *know* at the beginning. We knew you and Martyn were dating when Costello wasn't around. You used my son."

"I didn't *use* Martyn," Charlotte said sadly. "I thought he was my friend—"

"And threw in a little sex," Nicole broke in with malice. "You'd been getting plenty with Costello. You must have missed it when he was away. Martyn was there. He was stupid enough to stay in love with you. That's what you do, isn't it? *Use* men."

High time to announce his presence, Rohan decided— only Charlotte's answer riveted him to the spot.

"It was Martyn who used *me*, Nicole."

No mistaking the utter gravity of her tone.

"Which means exactly what?" Lesley Prescott barked out. "You got caught out, didn't you? You never meant to fall pregnant by my son. It was always Costello you wanted."

"Always," Charlotte agreed. "How could I possibly have turned to Martyn after Rohan? Martyn was a liar. Lying was part of his nature. And it started early. It was Martyn who challenged Mattie to swim the river."

"Oh, yeah!" Nicole burst out, ample chest heaving.

"You knew your brother more than you care to admit, Nicole. You *know* he hit me. Not in the early years, but towards the end, when he was so unhappy. You *know*, but you don't dare speak the truth in front of your mother."

Lesley Prescott's face, like Charlotte's, was showing the depth of her upset. "Now it's your turn to lie," she cried. "My son would *never* do such a thing. I never saw any evidence of abuse. It wouldn't have been tolerated. Martyn adored you, even when he was off with women hardly more than prostitutes."

"It doesn't matter now, Lesley. I'm sorry I told you." Charlotte gave vent to a weary sigh.

"If my son struck you, you must have deserved it." Lesley Prescott launched into mitigation. In truth, she was shocked by the idea Martyn might have struck his beautiful wife. "You were withholding your marital obligations. You weren't a proper wife to him. Did you never consider he had saved you from a scandal? He *married* you. He thought the child was his. We all did.'

"I did too, Lesley," Charlotte responded soberly. "I was so ill-informed in those days I made a huge mistake. Rohan remains the love of my life. I was on the pill when I was with him. We couldn't afford for me to fall pregnant. I didn't realise at the time things can go wrong. I had a bout of sickness that interfered with the efficacy of the pill. I didn't know then. I know now."

"So you didn't take the pill with Martyn? Is that it?" Lesley scoffed, unable to abandon the pretence that her son had been perfect.

"With Rohan away, I stopped. There was no reason to keep on taking it until Rohan returned."

"What a risk you took with Martyn, then!" Lesley said bitterly. "You fed off his admiration and love. You seduced him, didn't you?"

"You were missing all that hot sex." Nicole, who had never had sex —hot or cold— laughed crudely.

"Do shut up, Nicole. Get a life. *Do* something about yourself," Charlotte told her—not without pity. She turned to her ex mother-in-law. "I'm truly sorry, Lesley, for all the tragic things that have happened. I grieved for Martyn too, you know."

Lesley glared at her darkly. "Rubbish! In the olden days, Charlotte Marsdon, you would have been burned at the stake."

Something in Rohan snapped. He moved swiftly, the heart torn out of him.

"Look me in the face and tell me you're lying!" Lesley Prescott was crying. "You seduced my son. You probably got a huge kick out of it. After all, he worshipped the ground you walked on. You had to have *him* too."

Charlotte spoke so quietly Rohan could barely hear what she was saying. Then it hit him with horrified amazement.

"Martyn raped me."

He staggered as if at a king hit.

Martyn, their friend from early childhood, had raped her?

Inside the room Lesley Prescott was going berserk, also

horrified by *that* word. "Liar!" she shouted, waving her arms wildly in the air.

"What do *you* think, Nicole?" Charlotte gave the younger woman a chance to redeem herself. "You're the *one* person who knows what Martyn was like. Rohan doesn't know. I was too ashamed to tell him."

"Good!" Nicole actually looked a little crazy. "Why didn't you watch out for him, you fool?"

Lesley Prescott made a yelping sound, rounding on her daughter, astounded. "What in God's name are you talking about?"

"Wake up, Mum," Nicole said with undisguised contempt. "You and your Martyn. Your can-do-no-wrong son. Martyn was a bastard. I *knew* he was hitting Charlotte. It must have been awful for her. I *knew* he'd forced sex on her. He *told* me. He boasted about it. How else was he going to get her away from Rohan Costello?"

So there it is, Rohan's inner voice said. *The direst of secrets revealed.*

Hot blood rose like a tide, forming a red mist before his eyes. *His beautiful Charlotte.* He hadn't been there to protect or defend her. She would have trusted Martyn. If Martyn weren't dead, he thought he would kill him.

Eyes ablaze, Rohan rapped hard on the glass door with his knuckles, startling all three women. They turned their heads in unison, all three appalled.

"What a contemptible creature you are, Nicole," he said. "In your own way you're as guilty as your cowardly brother. Time to go, Charlotte." He issued the command. "I told you not to come here without me. These people have never done you any good."

Lesley Prescott felt intimidated to the bone. When exactly had young Rohan Costello become such a commanding figure? "How dare you come into my home unannounced?" she asked hoarsely.

"That wasn't my intention, Mrs Prescott. Only one never knows what one might learn by staying out of sight. I'd intended to announce myself—only in following your riveting conversation I have been able to learn the truth. Charlotte was protecting your sick bully of a son, Mrs Prescott. Think of the nobility of that. She kept silent. A mother herself, she didn't want to hurt *you*. You can only blame yourself for provoking her now. And I'm glad. Because now we have the truth of why Charlotte married Martyn. She believed herself pregnant by him. She believed marrying him was the proper course to take. Her parents failed her. *I* failed her—going so far away, leaving cunning, manipulative Martyn to seize his moment. It was always his way. Charlotte provided a few clues along the way, but I was so self-involved I was blind to them. Martyn was a coward, and a traitor to our lifelong friendship."

As Rohan moved further into the room both Prescott women stumbled back.

When exactly had Martyn turned bad? Lesley Prescott asked herself. How much of it was her fault? "Martyn is dead," she said, her face contorted with pain.

It took everything Rohan had to fall back on forgiveness. For the mother. Not the son. "Despite all the pain Martyn inflicted on us, Mrs Prescott, Charlotte and I *are* saddened by that. Come here to me, Charlotte." He held out an imperative hand.

Charlotte rushed to him, desperate for his comfort.

"The Valley will never accept you," Lesley Prescott told them heavily.

Rohan returned her a cool, confident look. "You're wrong about that, Mrs Prescott. I have big plans for the Valley. My enterprises will be creating a lot of jobs, and the von Luckners have come on board with their great expertise. Charlotte Vale will be producing ultra-premium wines. I have plans for the olive groves as well. Plans for a first-class restaurant. I think you'll find the Valley more than happy about it all after they absorb the initial shock that Christopher is my son. But then, I think a lot of people already know. We really should present some sort of a united front, Mrs Prescott. Charlotte and I want no enmity. The *one* person you should be angry at—the *one* person who betrayed us all—is Martyn. And your daughter definitely needs counselling. Jealousy is a cancer. She needs treatment. Neither of you should want to make an enemy of me," he warned, his hand tightening on Charlotte's. "Time to leave, Charlotte. It's over now."

"Are you okay to drive?" Rohan asked as they walked to her car. She was as pale as a lily.

"I'm fine, Rohan. Don't worry about me." She looked away to her father's Mercedes. "Dad lent it to you?"

"No problem. I took the chopper from Sydney. I was anxious about you. What time do you pick up Christopher?" He opened her car door, waiting for her to get behind the wheel.

"I'm always there ten minutes early, so two-fifty."

"I'll come with you. Follow me back to Riverbend."

She should have felt as if a great burden had been lifted from her shoulders. Instead she wondered what Rohan thought of her under his mask of gentleness and concern. However much he understood, his respect for her would have plummeted. She had never intended to tell him what Martyn had done. She had wanted to keep her self-respect.

It was well-documented the world over that innocent victims of abuse—physical and mental—can feel an irrational, yet powerful sense of guilt.

Charlotte had been one of them—much like an abused child. But the dark cloud that had hung over her for so long was about to be totally dispersed.

Mrs Burch opened the front door. She looked surprised to see them, noting with concern that both of them looked what she later described to her husband as "traumatised".

"Tea, thank you, Louise." Rohan kept a steadying hand on Charlotte. "We'll have it in the library."

Mrs Burch hurried away. All sorts of strange things were happening in the Valley. Beautiful Charlotte Prescott was clearly in shock. But if she was in any kind of trouble she had come to the right man.

Mrs Burch soon returned, wheeling a trolley set with tea things and a plate of home-baked cookies. She withdrew quietly, shutting the library door after her.

Rohan poured Charlotte a cup of tea. He added a little milk and two teaspoons of sugar, even though he knew she didn't take sugar in her tea. "Drink it down."

She responded with a quiet little smile.

Rohan took his tea black, but at the last moment added a teaspoon of sugar. "I need it," he said laconically, sinking into one of the burgundy leather armchairs that surrounded a reading table.

He allowed Charlotte to finish her tea in peace, then took the cup and saucer from her, leading her to the sofa.

"You're in no way to blame, Charlotte." He covered her hands with his own. "As I said to Mrs Prescott, we all failed you when you desperately needed help. I should accept the blame as I never considered for a moment that Martyn would force himself on you. My trust in him was woefully misplaced. Martyn always had his problems, but

I never believed he would hurt you. What a fool I've been!"
He sighed deeply. "The closest friends have been known to
turn into aggressors, even murderers. But Martyn! What a
catastrophe! You didn't think to let me know?"

She didn't lift her head, though relief was intensifying
in her.

"You didn't think to go to my mother?" he continued,
stroking her hand. "I know you couldn't go to *yours*!"

Charlotte spoke up. "I began to experience morning
sickness very early on, Rohan. I knew what was happening
to me. I believed I was pregnant by Martyn. How could I
let *you* of all people know? I had betrayed our love. How
could I go to your mother, tell her I was carrying Martyn
Prescott's baby? I could never put voice to the fact he had
forced me. I was suffering such shame. I *did* know Martyn
had always been in love with me. I felt I *should* have fore-
seen the danger. Afterwards he couldn't have been more
contrite. More sad and sorry."

"They *all* are!" Rohan said grimly.

"I suppose… Martyn broke down in tears, begging me
to forgive him. I tried hard, but I *did* keep some part of
myself remote."

"The sad and sorry bit doesn't jell with Nicole's damning
comments."

"No. But he *did* need my love, Rohan. He begged for it.
I tried to enter his world. It was a disaster. As time went
on his attitude changed. Became belligerent."

"He began to hit you." Rohan was barely holding down
his rage. "How low can a man sink? But then he wasn't a
man, was he?"

"In many ways he was like a greedy child who needed
instant gratification. But what he did weighed very heavily
on him I think."

Rohan couldn't conceal his disgust. "Stop making excuses for Martyn, Charlotte."

She looked into his blazing eyes. "Maybe it lessens *my* guilt."

"*No* guilt." Rohan gave his verdict.

"Any number of girls and women are brave enough to go it alone."

"And any number *aren't*. Not at eighteen, without support. I realise how frightened you must have been. How trapped. You had to endure years of being victimised by Martyn. You couldn't tell your father? Even Gordon Prescott? He would never have countenanced abuse. Nicole shouldn't have either. That woman needs a good psychiatrist."

"Maybe I do too."

"So does anyone who suffers abuse in silence." His voice was as gentle as any man's could be. "Forgive me for making moral judgements, my love. You were trying to tell me. I was too full of my own griefs. I love you, Charlotte. I've never stopped loving you. I gave you my heart. I don't want it back. We created our monster. His name was Martyn. Time now to lay poor Martyn to rest."

Rohan drew her to her feet. "Let's stroll down to the river. I feel like being out in the clean fresh air."

They walked hand in hand through the gardens, past the beds flushed with flowers, right down to the edge of the river. It sparkled in the sunshine, the glassy surface mantled with thousands of dancing sequins.

"If we could only go back in time," she said softly. "Mattie would be alive. You and I would be happily married. You would have asked Martyn to be your best man."

"A terrible irony in that!" He gathered her into his

embrace. "Don't let's speak of Martyn any more. Not in this place. We can never go back, however much we want to. What we *can* do is take control of our future. We're going to live it the way it would have been. Only better. We have one another. And we have our beautiful son. We're blessed. Do you love me, Charlotte?" He turned her face up to him, blue gaze intent.

"Heart and soul!" Her lovely smile was like a sunburst. "I've been so *alone* without you."

He held her to him. "We're together now. You have nothing and no one to fear. The sad years are over. A few hurdles won't go away like magic, but we'll contend with them. Believe me?" he asked.

"My belief in you has never wavered, Rohan," she answered without hesitation. "I can handle anything with you by my side." She paused, then added a little shakily, "I thought I would die of shame if you found out."

"Ah, *no*!" he groaned. "I love you, Charlotte. I'll always take care of you." He bent his head, touching his forehead to hers, then he kissed her so sweetly, so deeply, so passionately, the tormented element within her broke like a severed twine. "We have peace now, Charlotte," he murmured. "We have our whole lives. Ready to marry me?"

The world seemed bathed in a gorgeous brightness. It was as though the sun, moon and stars had come out together. *"I can't wait!"* she cried ecstatically.

Above them in the trees an invisible bird began to sing. The sound was so beautiful, so flute-like, so poignant, so far-carrying it seemed to travel the length and breadth of the river.

"Do you suppose that's Mattie?" Rohan asked, lifting his head.

Charlotte too was filled with such a sense of wonder she was nearly weeping. She stared above her into the green density of leaves. Hard to see a bird, but there was such a *glow*. It was spilling out of the trees. Pouring over them. "Why not?" she breathed.

Mattie wasn't really dead. He was an angel.

"Who knows what forces are at work in this universe?" Rohan mused, putting his arm around her slender shoulders. "We should be getting back, my love. It's almost time to pick up our son."

Its song completed, the invisible bird rose up into the sky on opalescent wings. It made a full circuit around Charlotte and Rohan before it disappeared.

Had it even been there?

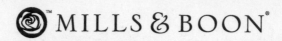

MILLS & BOON®

JANUARY 2011 HARDBACK TITLES

ROMANCE

Hidden Mistress, Public Wife	Emma Darcy
Jordan St Claire: Dark and Dangerous	Carole Mortimer
The Forbidden Innocent	Sharon Kendrick
Bound to the Greek	Kate Hewitt
The Secretary's Scandalous Secret	Cathy Williams
Ruthless Boss, Dream Baby	Susan Stephens
Prince Voronov's Virgin	Lynn Raye Harris
Mistress, Mother...Wife?	Maggie Cox
With This Fling...	Kelly Hunter
Girls' Guide to Flirting with Danger	Kimberly Lang
Wealthy Australian, Secret Son	Margaret Way
A Winter Proposal	Lucy Gordon
His Diamond Bride	Lucy Gordon
Surprise: Outback Proposal	Jennie Adams
Juggling Briefcase & Baby	Jessica Hart
Deserted Island, Dreamy Ex!	Nicola Marsh
Rescued by the Dreamy Doc	Amy Andrews
Navy Officer to Family Man	Emily Forbes

HISTORICAL

Lady Folbroke's Delicious Deception	Christine Merrill
Breaking the Governess's Rules	Michelle Styles
Her Dark and Dangerous Lord	Anne Herries
How To Marry a Rake	Deb Marlowe

MEDICAL™

Sheikh, Children's Doctor...Husband	Meredith Webber
Six-Week Marriage Miracle	Jessica Matthews
St Piran's: Italian Surgeon, Forbidden Bride	Margaret McDonagh
The Baby Who Stole the Doctor's Heart	Dianne Drake

1210 Gen Std LP

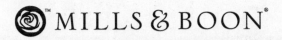

MILLS & BOON®

JANUARY 2011 LARGE PRINT TITLES

ROMANCE

A Stormy Greek Marriage	Lynne Graham
Unworldly Secretary, Untamed Greek	Kim Lawrence
The Sabbides Secret Baby	Jacqueline Baird
The Undoing of de Luca	Kate Hewitt
Cattle Baron Needs a Bride	Margaret Way
Passionate Chef, Ice Queen Boss	Jennie Adams
Sparks Fly with Mr Mayor	Teresa Carpenter
Rescued in a Wedding Dress	Cara Colter

HISTORICAL

Vicar's Daughter to Viscount's Lady	Louise Allen
Chivalrous Rake, Scandalous Lady	Mary Brendan
The Lord's Forced Bride	Anne Herries
Wanted: Mail-Order Mistress	Deborah Hale

MEDICAL™

Dare She Date the Dreamy Doc?	Sarah Morgan
Dr Drop-Dead Gorgeous	Emily Forbes
Her Brooding Italian Surgeon	Fiona Lowe
A Father for Baby Rose	Margaret Barker
Neurosurgeon . . . and Mum!	Kate Hardy
Wedding in Darling Downs	Leah Martyn

MILLS & BOON

FEBRUARY 2011 HARDBACK TITLES

ROMANCE

Flora's Defiance	Lynne Graham
The Reluctant Duke	Carole Mortimer
The Wedding Charade	Melanie Milburne
The Devil Wears Kolovsky	Carol Marinelli
His Unknown Heir	Chantelle Shaw
Princess From the Past	Caitlin Crews
The Inherited Bride	Maisey Yates
Interview with a Playboy	Kathryn Ross
Walk on the Wild Side	Natalie Anderson
Do Not Disturb	Anna Cleary
The Nanny and the CEO	Rebecca Winters
Crown Prince, Pregnant Bride!	Raye Morgan
Friends to Forever	Nikki Logan
Beauty and the Brooding Boss	Barbara Wallace
Three Weddings and a Baby	Fiona Harper
The Last Summer of Being Single	Nina Harrington
Single Dad's Triple Trouble	Fiona Lowe
Midwife, Mother…Italian's Wife	Fiona McArthur

HISTORICAL

Miss in a Man's World	Anne Ashley
Captain Corcoran's Hoyden Bride	Annie Burrows
His Counterfeit Condesa	Joanna Fulford
Rebellious Rake, Innocent Governess	Elizabeth Beacon

MEDICAL™

Cedar Bluff's Most Eligible Bachelor	Laura Iding
Doctor: Diamond in the Rough	Lucy Clark
Becoming Dr Bellini's Bride	Joanna Neil
St Piran's: Daredevil, Doctor…Dad!	Anne Fraser

0111 Gen Std LP

MILLS & BOON®

FEBRUARY 2011 LARGE PRINT TITLES

ROMANCE

HISTORICAL

MEDICAL™